JACK WEST

ADVENTURES

THE MAGIC POND

Perry D. DeFiore

JACK WEST

ADVENTURES

THE MAGIC POND

Perry D. DeFiore

Contents

Prologue

The loud thump from his heart came in so loud and heavy it was hard to hear anything else around him. Adrenaline rushed through his body propelling him to go faster, yet the prickling pain in his lungs burned as hot cinders rekindling with every breath, telling him he couldn't go much further. Branches gashed his limbs as he fought to make his way through, blood leaving more evidence of the trail for his pursuer. He had no plan to escape this, there hadn't been any time to think of one, all he could for now was run, but that alone seemed futile in the end.

Jack was in trouble, and he had to do something to escape or conquer over his hunter. Running for his life it was hard to think of the path that landed him here; the speed of his footsteps over the hard terrain turned into a slow motion blur replaced by an easy stride over a paved street; one he knew well, one that had a sense of safety; his home street.

CHAPTER 1

School's Out

School is sometimes such a bore
They always want you to learn and do more
But vacations are great
We wait like horses at the gate
To pounce on things to do
Having experiences anew

"Hey, Jack." Red gently brought his fist to Jack's in salutation.

"Hey, Red," Jack smiled.

"Last day, thank God!"

"Yeah. Bet you're glad, too. You're leaving to-morrow, right?"

"Cancun, here I come! White beaches, clear warm blue water, and tons of girls in bikinis." Red's large round brown eyes seemed to clash with his red hair, like they just didn't belong there.

Adolescence is that wonderful age when boys begin to notice girls, usually starting out shy and timid, but Red seemed to have skipped the faint-heartedness while Jack was still a little bashful and fearful of getting involved with the opposite sex.

"Wish I could tag along," Jack smiled, shaking his head slightly. He was used to Red's references to girls all the time, but it was a little more than comical because he had never actually seen Red with a girl, at least not alone with one, anyway. Then Jack's smile faded. "Just couldn't convince my parents to let me go."

"Parents suck. I asked mine to talk to your parents for you. I think they did, but maybe your parents didn't have enough dough. I'm taking my small binoculars. Maybe I'll get a chance to sneak off on my own when we get to the beach. Get some real sights, know what I mean? Wanna see up close. Anyway, it's only for a week. We'll go to the water park after I get back. Already got my season pass. You?"

Red always did that. He rambled and mixed his conversations without stopping, as if his mind jumped around a lot, so it could be hard to follow him sometimes. It literally drove the teachers crazy. Before you could answer one of his questions, he'd come up with another one or make some other unrelated comment.

Red—Garret Fitzgerald, was labeled Red because of his hair, it was so fiery red you couldn't help but notice—a blessing from his father. The girls found his freckle-face attractive. He was tall for his age, which helped him be one of the best receivers, as tight end, on the school's football team. Jack was two inches shorter than Red, but more muscular and stronger. He was a first string running back. The coach wanted him to play quarterback, but Jack did everything he could to avoid that position—too much pressure. Fans always blamed everything, especially the losses on the quarterback, and his school wasn't exactly number one. Besides, the quarterback had to know everyone's plays, not that Jack couldn't memorize them; it was just that he believed there were other things more important to concentrate on.

Jack and Garret had met some five years ago, on the day Jack moved into the neighborhood. He had noticed a redheaded kid sitting inside the opened-door garage, in a house at the very center of the Cul-de-Sac, while carrying boxes from the orange and white moving truck. Jack and his dad were about half way through unloading the truck when Garret showed up and introduced himself as Red. Jack's first impression was that Red dyed his hair, given its bright neon sign-like color. Then, without speaking a word, Red grabbed one of the boxes and just began carrying them into the house. Red was like that, very spontaneous, doing things without thinking and sometimes without considering the consequences of his actions. The two became best of friends from that moment on.

"Yeah," said Jack, "My Mom already gave me the pass. My dad's gotta work. I think they're planning on a trip to Los Angeles or something like that. Hey, you didn't leave any subjects, did you?" working hard to change the subject nonchalantly.

"72 in Algebra. 70 in History. Rest were 75 to 80, well, 100 in PE."

Jack laughed, "Well, at least you passed. No summer classes this year."

"Thank God! Not everyone's a brain like you."

"School's easy, that's all," Jack shrugged, a little embarrassed by his friend's comment. Jack found school not to be much of a challenge, academically. His dad always told him that school would become more challenging later, especially in college. In the meantime, Jack spent his free time on the internet learning about the universe. He was especially curious about the black holes and the gravitational forces that held everything in place; and was fascinated with how the Sun, the planets, and the whole galaxy flew around in space at very high rates of speed and no one even seemed to notice we were moving.

"Easy for *you* to say. Signed up for football?"

"Oh yeah. Wouldn't miss that for anything. No way." Football was a passion that was shared by both Red and Jack, and the sport was instrumental in the development of their relationship. "Coach said we start practice on August 5th, right? Hope your parents consider that when they plan their vacation." Red blurted.

"I know. I told them. They said August is still a long ways off. We're gonna have a lot of pounds to sweat off from this summer."

"Not you. You're always working out," Red laughed.

Red was right. Jack had a treadmill in his bedroom and he used it faithfully. Running almost every morning before breakfast.

Jack and Red lived in a small, quiet community next to the school. The school did not provide bus service to their neighborhood because of its proximity, so they walked to school every day. Many kids in the neighborhood rode their bikes. But, not Jack or Red, they enjoyed the 'walk and talk', both to and from school.

The early June afternoon sun sent its heat down hard and there was not even a light breeze around to reduce its intensity, but the two young men didn't seem to mind or even notice the dripping perspiration that began to form as they chatted walking up their street. Red mostly talked about girls and Jack mostly smiled and listened with an occasional comment about any other subject.

Sometimes Jack tried to talk about the universe, but Red would always quickly change the subject thirty or so seconds into the topic, preferring to talk sports, girls or the weekend. Jack found it difficult sharing his interest with anyone at school, especially the girls—they had a reputation of being smarter than the guys in class, but also because he had a hard time expressing himself around girls. Even his science teacher seemed to avoid getting into discussions with him.

"Yeah. Well... We're home. Have a great trip, Red. I am sure you will have a blast. Send me a postcard and let me know how the beaches are. Still wish I was going." Jack waved at his friend as he walked up the driveway to his three-bedroom red brick home.

"Thanks, man. And don't worry, I'll kiss at least one girl for you," Red yelled as he continued up the street. "And another few more for me," he smirked.

"Yeah, right!" Jack chuckled and shook his head as he keyed in the code on the garage door opener. Jack opened the door to the kitchen after pressing the square white button to close the garage door. He stepped into a cool sea of air that felt so delicious he had to stop a second to enjoy the pleasure.

His parents wouldn't be home. Jack's Mom was a bank manager and got home at 6:10pm every day like clockwork, Monday through Friday. His Dad was an executive for a large chemical company, which made him travel constantly. He usually left every Sunday night for a new destination and came back on Friday evenings. Sometimes he waited until Monday morning to leave, depending on how far away he was going.

Jack slipped his backpack off and let it fall onto the couch, a sudden refreshing coolness on his back brought a smile, and then he pulled his phone out to call his Mom, a daily routine on weekdays. "Hi, Mom."

"Hi Honey. How was your last day of school?"

"Boring!"

His Mother just nodded on the other end. She knew it was hard for life not to be boring for her son. "No party in school?"

"Well, we tried, but you can't really do anything at school, so we just sat around and waited for the time to pass, munching on some snacks that someone's mom sent. No food fights or anything, boring!"

"That poor mother, going through all that trouble to send the snacks. And thank goodness you weren't involved in any food fights! Being expelled, especially on the last day of school, could give me heartburn. There's spaghetti in the fridge, Sweetheart. Just heat it up in the microwave for two minutes. That should hold you over till dinner."

"Okay."

"And wash the dishes, please."

"Yes, ma'am." he said rolling his eyes.

"Gotta go. See you soon, Dear."

He nodded and watched the connection end on the screen of his cell phone. He smiled. *"Won't have to do that for a couple of months now,"* he thought with a smile.

He opened the fridge and stared into the cluster of containers that filled every shelf; shuffled through

them until he saw the clear container with the white
worms in red sauce, then debated whether to heat it up
or go for some chicken quesadillas at Taco Bell a couple of blocks away from home.

Jack sighed a lazy sigh and grabbed the container
of spaghetti. He heated up the food and went to his
room to eat and play video games. There were usually
about eight guys online that joined him in the games,
always at different times depending on when they got
home and how soon they could escape their parents, a
topic of much discussion at school. Now they had the
summer, and all day to play.

He was losing to one of his friends, time passing
quickly, when suddenly he heard the front door and
glanced at his clock on the nightstand. The red numbers beamed 6:10. He jumped up off the bed and
quickly put the empty dish under his bed.

"Jack! I'm home!" his Mother yelled.

He knew she would typically go to her room,
change, and then go to the kitchen to fix dinner, but
occasionally she would come directly to his room to
say hello. He glanced out his bedroom door and saw
the coast was clear. He grabbed the dirty dishes from
under his bed and quickly slipped downstairs, placing
them in the sink. Realizing he had left the grated
cheese out Jack flipped towards it, swiftly placed it
back in the fridge and plopped himself down on the
brown leather living room sofa turning on the TV.

"Jack! Why didn't you wash your dishes?" His Mother yelled some fifteen minutes later.

"Uh, sorry Mom, I forgot. You're gonna cook dinner now anyway, aren't you?"

"I'm not your maid, young man. You come wash this container and silverware right now."

"Yes, ma'am." *I should have left everything under the bed till tomorrow.* chimed the voice in his head. He dragged himself off of the couch and strolled his way into the kitchen. *At least I escaped her finding out about eating upstairs. She really would've gone ape on me.* came the afterthought. Eating in his room was one of Jack's Mother's big 'no, no's'.

"So what are your plans with all the free time this summer, Dear?" His Mother asked cheerfully as she busied herself peeling potatoes and cutting them into french fries.

Jack walked over to the light brown wooden kitchen table and slid into one of the chairs. His Mother had changed into her gray University of Texas shirt and a pair of blue jeans. Her blonde hair was cut short with the sides tapered into a point. Jack had once overheard his dad remark on liking her hair better long, as it was when they first met, but Jack thought she looked better than most other moms.

"Oh, good. You're making fries. And I don't know, Mom. Red and I will probably go to the water park a lot when he gets back from Cancun."

"There are Boy Scout camps and other summer camps I saw in the paper and internet. I'm sure your Father will be okay with the cost." She didn't really care for Red and had nixed Jack from going to Cancun with his family. She didn't trust Red. Something about him, although she really could not put her finger on it, told her that he was trouble.

"I think I'll pass, Mom. And I'm not a Boy Scout, anyway. Besides, I really cannot see myself sitting around and tying knots with a bunch of other guys, either. What else you making?"

"Hamburgers and baked beans. Saw your grades. Good job! The only thing you didn't get a 95 or above in was Language Arts. What happened there?" She turned and gave him a short stare with her big blue eyes , then went back to her dinner preparations.

"Teacher had it in for me."

She stopped forming the hamburger into patties, holding a chunk of meat in her right hand, and looked at Jack again.

"Aw, c'mon, Jack. Teachers don't have it in for you—unless, maybe you were causing a problem in class?"

"I'm for real, Mom. She doesn't like anyone disa- greeing with her opinions. In some cases, I challenged her about the meanings of the stories. If you don't agree with her, you're just wrong."

"Some cases? Or maybe all of them."

Jack smiled and shrugged his shoulders.

"Thought so. And you weren't smart enough to just agree with her like the rest of the class?"

"But she was wrong, Mom. I'm not going to be one of her puppets. I have the right to my own opinion, don't I?"

"Well. That 88 would have probably been a 98 if you had just gone along with her."

"Probably, but it's still not right," Jack muttered.

She shook her head, smiling, and went back to her cooking. She knew her son was just like his Father. Jack always saw more in situations than most people, including herself, and was like a rock in his opinions. That trait is what made his Father so successful.

"Your Father will probably agree with you." She said softly, smiling to herself and shaking her head slightly.

"He's never around," Jack complained.

"Jack! Your Father is home every weekend!" This was getting to be a frequent comment lately. Last year, her husband had taken a new position with increased responsibilities resulting in a lot more travel. The family had somewhat regretted his accepting the promotion, but it was hard to turn down the huge salary increase.

Jack simply nodded in silence, taking in the smell of cigarettes coming from his Mother's direction, reminding him of the smells of alcohol he knew would follow. He rose from his chair and went back to the couch landing onto the cushion with a sigh.

This is going to be a long summer, he thought to himself, *What am I going to do this summer? Especially this next week until Red gets back.*

Red made things fun! He was always spontaneous and often thought of something for the both of them to do, even if it sometimes got them into trouble. Red was a risk taker and Jack was the one always getting them 'out' of trouble.

Jack nodded to himself contemplating his plan for tomorrow. He would do what he always did when wanting to be alone and think about something—go to his secret place, his very own think tank. This was a magical place in its own sort of way, where Jack could yell at the top of his lungs and no one would hear. He could yell out profanity and no one would know or care for that matter. Although, Jack was never really into cursing. He had been impressed by his grandfather's famous words, "profanity is a sign of a person's ignorance." Of course, Jack could never share with anyone his true feelings, lest he be made fun of by his friends, so, in an attempt to fit in with 'the guys', he would let out a word or two when he was with them.

His secret place was a place where he could sit alone and analyze his life, where he could relax not worrying about parents, friends, teachers or anyone. He could clear his mind and do absolutely nothing if that was what he wanted. He loved visiting his secret place. *Yes*, he nodded to himself, tomorrow he would go there.

CHAPTER 2

Meagan

Parents are such a drag
All they do is nag
Do these chores and that
They just don't know where it's at

"Meagan! Where do you think you're going, young lady?"

The familiar, but strange, feeling of 'caught grabbing' on her chest froze Meagan into a stop so sudden that she nearly splattered onto the white wooden door to freedom.

"Shoot!" came the whisper, louder than she'd hoped, "Aw, Mom. It's Saturday and school's out." Megan turned to see a fair-skinned "Superwoman" standing with her legs spread, fists on her hips, glaring at her with blue eyes that could pierce through someone's brain. Her long golden wavy hair rested on her shoulders. Meagan could picture the big red S across her Mother's chest and the long red cape gently blowing in the breeze behind her.

"Chores first, young lady. The garage. Now."

"Yes, ma'am," she said in a defeated voice. Meagan let her backpack slide off her shoulders and heard it plunk on the floor, and then worked her way past her Mother to the dark dungeon called the garage.

Meagan sighed as she began to put away her Father's tools so she could clean the workbench.

I don't know why I have to do this. These are not my tools, I didn't put them here. I have to clean my room. If I make a mess, I have to clean it up. It's not fair, she complained to herself while she worked.

She arranged the tools her Dad had left on the bench in the handmade wooden cabinets where every screwdriver, every wrench, every hammer, every everything had its place. After finishing the workbench, Meagan picked up a few more items that were out of place, and then swept the garage. The whole mess only took her forty-five minutes. She looked around and nodded to herself. *Done!*

Meagan opened the door that connected the garage and the kitchen and quietly walked in. The cool AC felt refreshing after all that time spent slaving in the dungeon. She stopped and listened. The house was so quiet she could almost think it was empty, but she knew better. She silently moved to the front door where she had left her backpack, grabbed it by the straps and then quietly made her way back to the garage, looking and listening carefully for her Mother with each step.

Once in the garage with the kitchen door closed, she gave a sigh of relief and slipped her backpack onto her back. As briskly and quietly as she could, she walked out of the garage, keyed in the code to close it, and continued down the driveway. With one quick glance back over her shoulder to make sure that the coast was clear, she broke into a run down the short street.

Beneath her stride the street ended as if someone had run out of concrete and just didn't bother to complete the job, or maybe they could not afford to buy more. About fifty yards further, from the end of the street and over a field of grass, stood 'the woods'. As soon as she got past the first tree she hid behind it and looked down the street hoping that no one had noticed her. Meagan's eyes narrowed at the scenery; there were only five homes on each side of the single street. It reminded Meagan of a picture from a magazine, a small street with a handful of homes of European architecture and beautifully trimmed yards of dark green Bermuda grass with tall trees in their back yards.

Her dad had built this neighborhood about eight years ago. He was an independent contractor who worked for two different construction companies. He worked many Saturdays, but usually just in the mornings, when he paid the workers. Meagan's dad was always building something in the garage. He enjoyed building furniture, and had made most of theirs. Meagan had to admit; her Father was an excellent carpenter and there wasn't anything that he could not build with his own hands.

Her Mother worked at the electric company, Monday through Friday, from 7:00am to 4:00pm. At least one of her parents was almost always home when she was.

Sundays were church days. Meagan hated having to wake up early and despised dressing in her Sunday's Best just to go sit on some hard wooden bench to listen to the preacher talk. The sermon always made her sleepy. Her Mother was continually poking her in the arm with an elbow, keeping her awake. Church could be *such a bore*. The sermon always seemed to drag on for an eternity. Her dad sat on her side and Meagan noticed how he fought the same desire to occasionally nod off.

After church, they usually went to the pancake house for breakfast where Meagan would always find at least a couple of her friends; that was the good part of Sunday. Once home, Meagan would immediately slip into her jeans and a t-shirt and make her way to 'the woods', except during football season. From mid-August until February, Sunday afternoons were great. The whole family was a football enthusiast and everyone sat in front of the television with snacks, dips and drinks to watch the game. Sometimes, Dad suggested going to a sports bar so they could see all the games playing at the same time, though Mom insisted they make it a family event at home. Meagan's Mom had hidden reasons. Her Dad liked to drink and did so a lot more when they went to a sports bar. Not that her Mother didn't drink, she just drank less. The cigarette smoke smell that hung heavy in the large room of televisions grossed Meagan, despite the flair of the multiple Sunday games display. .

Meagan's interests were different than most other girls. She loved collecting insects and inspecting them under the microscope she kept in her bedroom. Her Mother hated that, but her dad always thought she would grow out of it, so he was continually telling her Mother to leave her alone. Meagan hoped he wouldn't change his mind. She was fascinated with the way a fly's wings were made and thought it so cool that spiders had all these eyes on the tops of their heads. She tried to imagine humans having eyes like that. There would be no need to turn their heads to see behind. That would certainly make it easier for the receivers on the 49ers team to catch those long passes.

Meagan was glad to be out of the house. She continued to observe the neighborhood from behind the tree. Not a single soul was stirring, not one car parked in a driveway or driving down the street. It was as if the whole neighborhood was deserted. Meagan turned

with a huge grin across her face and made her way into
the woods; to her very own special place, known only
be her. Her backpack felt heavy with all the supplies
she had brought and it wasn't long before her back
was wet with perspiration, but with every step she
took, she moved further away from the grim of Saturday's that tugged at her insides. Meagan wasn't always happy with her home life. Her parents frequently
joined their friends out on Saturday nights and did not
return home until very late with a stench of beer and
cigarettes that impregnated the entire house. Meagan
hated that. And it seemed though that her mom would
compensate the wrong by busying Meagan with an
endless list of chores, like washing the dishes, vacu-
uming the carpet, taking out the garbage, and dusting
the furniture.

The woods felt cool and the tall pines engulfed her
with a pleasant fragrance. She looked up at the thousands of pine needles that blocked most of the hot sun.
The red maples gave even more shade and whispered
to her in the gentle breeze. She smiled. Meagan could
not be happier that her Father had picked this street to
live on.

Though the view above her head was always mesmerizing, the world beneath her feet never failed to
pull her eyes down. Curiosity always lurked under-
neath big rocks, which also caused the occasional tripping. Today Meagan's trip found her an unusually
large centipede under the proverbial tripping rock. She

scrambled and reached for her Ziploc bag to trap it. She always kept sandwich bags and baby food jars in her backpack for new specimens. She sat looking at the specimen, admiring its blue jaws, or forcipules. She hadn't seen this species before. Not wanting to risk losing it and because centipedes can be dangerous she would have to go home first and put her specimen away. Then she would return to her secret place. There was still plenty of time.

CHAPTER 3

Tunnel of Light

Magic, magic of my pond
Into you I plunge my frustrations
Please, please raise your magic wand
And give me adventures and revelations

Jack's eyelids wanted to open, but he told them to stay shut, he had promised himself to sleep in till noon, but the light bathed him in its morning glory, tugged at him and pried his eyelids open. He opened his eyes, stared at the ceiling a few seconds, then sat up in bed. He had left the blinds open and the daylight was just creeping over the horizon, the sun would show its face in only minutes. Jack sighed and guessed he was just too used to getting up early for school. A noise brought his attention to the window and he saw his neighbor building one of those play houses with swings and a slide. He was wide-awake now, so he got dressed and went downstairs to find something to eat.

While he ate his cereal, Jack pondered on what he was going to take with him. He finished his breakfast, grudgingly washed his bowl and spoon, and then grabbed his backpack from the living room where he had left it the night before. *Good thing Mom didn't notice, she would have flipped out and yelled at me.* After emptying the backpack on the coffee table, Jack packed a pair of swimming trunks, some snacks and two bottles of water. He wouldn't need a towel. It was hot enough to dry off in the sun.

He hoisted the backpack onto his back and was about to leave, when he remembered to scoop up the things he left on the coffee table. He dropped them off on a shelf in the garage before he left the house, noticing various other items he had placed on the shelves over the last month, once again reminding himself to put all of it away when he got back

The street was quiet as he walked down it, making a usual and familiar turn towards his school, except today, he had no intention of stopping there, what a thought, *walk by and not to*. Behind his school was the track field, then the elementary school. A thick wooded area surrounded both schools and it was the edge of the woods beyond the elementary school to where his feet carried him with anxious anticipation. When Jack got to the corner of the woods, he turned and looked back to be sure no one was following him, then disappeared into the trees. After a few steps he turned and looked back again. No one was there. Jack was in his world now, on his way to his getaway place.

As he walked through the tall pines, maples and oaks, sometimes stumbling over branches that had fallen, he began to feel invigorated. For some reason hiking always made him feel stronger, his muscles felt like he was working out in the gym, and his lungs felt larger. He gazed up through the trees at the bits of light blue early June sky and took a deep breath through his nose, taking in the sweet smell of the pine trees and the leaves. *Oh, that really smelled good - nothing like his house, a host for lingering smells of beer and tobacco.* Jack felt the perspiration on his back, and the cool breeze on his forehead as it evaporated the beads of sweat.

A thought flashed through Jack's head as he walked towards his destination. He had a small tent from when his Dad, Mom, and he used to go camping, *before* they got too busy to spend any time with him. They had theirs, a bigger one, and Jack had his own, a small pup tent. He could live out here in the woods. He wondered how difficult it would be to get away with it. He sighed heavily, *don't think so, well , maybe.*

Jack arrived at his destination and looked at his cell phone. It had taken him only fifty minutes to get to the small lake, ten minutes less than usual. He smiled. He didn't know if this would be considered a lake, or large pond, perhaps it was simply a small one. What he did know was that he could throw a stone clear across it. He sat down on the thick fallen tree trunk he always sat on when he came here. Jack pulled his backpack off and set it on the ground behind him against the tree trunk. His back was soaking wet with sweat and he felt the sting of salt in the corner of his right eye. He wiped carefully, the sweat was a welcome trade off for his arrival. This was his sweet spot.

He came here any time of the year, even in winter when the cold blew bitterly through the leafless trees and bit into his cheeks and numbing his nose. Jack had always dreamt that someday the pond would freeze over and he could 'walk on water' or maybe play some solitary hockey with a tree limb and a stone. But he hadn't been that lucky yet, and it had been almost four years since he discovered this place. So much for living in South Texas. He was still waiting for that occasional snowstorm, obviously very occasional, maybe more like rare.

Jack loved it here at the pond. It was always so peaceful and tranquil. He could talk to himself, which he usually did. There was no one to make fun of him or say that he was crazy; call him stupid, irresponsible, or an idiot. Hurtful words that stayed with him, no matter how hard Jack tried to shake it off, words that entered through his parents, and at the football field.

Words that were mute here, squashed by the feeling of peace this place radiated.

There on the log, his arms propping his upper torso's weight, his legs stretched out in front of him, he looked at the water reflecting the images of the trees that surrounded it. The serenity brought an unconscious smile to his lips and he closed his eyes. The birds sang to each other—*he imagined maybe even to him,* and the rustling leaves whispered into his ears making it feel like someone was massaging his brain, making it relax.

There was something else very special about this place, mystical, magical, mesmerizing. He could feel it inside him. Jack was unable to explain the feelings; to describe it; or even comprehend it, but there was something pulling at his insides, calling him; something to do with the pond. He always felt it when he came here, ever since the first time. The water was always warm, more than warm, almost hot, even in the winter. Once, Jack brought a thermometer, borrowed from the lab, to test the temperature, which read thirty-two degrees Celsius. The thermometer didn't have Fahrenheit numbers on it, but Jack learned how to translate it by looking up the information on the internet. He calculated the water's temperature to be approximately ninety-two degrees. Sometimes, Jack would daydream of being an explorer of the history books who were famous for discovering some new land; however, he knew there was no new land to discover, not here on earth anyway. In some ways, this realization disappointed Jack.

It struck him that it felt as if the water was calling him; like a magnet pulling him in, urging him to follow, he could practically hear it. He reached around and pulled his backpack in front of him. Digging through it, Jack pulled out his gray track shorts he used as swimming trunks. *Why not,* he thought, *after all he had packed the shorts for swimming, had he not?* He had plenty of time on his hands now, hours. He had been coming here for a long time, but never actually gone into the water.

After changing into his shorts, he put his clothes in front of the log and put his backpack on top of it, just in case the wind picked up. Now barefoot, Jack carefully walked to the edge of the pond and took a couple of steps into the water. It was like stepping into a tub of hot water that was just right. The mud on the bottom was slippery and oozed through his toes. He smiled at how good it felt. In fact, he enjoyed it immensely. For so long the pond had called to him and he had resisted, fearing the unknown perhaps, but the luring call today was too strong to defy, and he felt like he was beginning a new adventure. Jack carefully continued a couple of steps at a time, until the water came up around his belly button. He waited without moving, staring into the water, until it cleared of the mud he had stirred up with his feet. There was a funny smell, as if someone had just lit a match or something similar. He brought his wet hand up to his nose and breathed in deeply. It definitely was the water. Whatever was in the water to make it smell like that, he assumed, also made it a little gray in color, although still clear enough to see to the bottom.

He bent his knees, sinking slowly until the water came up to his neck. It felt heavenly. A crazy desire to just lie down in it overcame Jack, and the next thing he knew, his head was submerged in the water. He opened his eyes, ever so slowly, until he was sure they didn't hurt. He could see fairly clearly, even though it was kind of weird looking through the grayish colored water, and he couldn't see very far in front of him. It was like looking through a fog.

He pushed off the bottom as gently as possible hoping to avoid stirring up the mud and swam out to the center of the pond using a breaststroke. It was deeper now, maybe twenty feet or so. Jack put his head into the water and could see the bottom pretty clearly. The muddy bottom had changed to what looked like thousands of small pebbles, and in the center they formed a sort of cone shaped hill. It resembled an ant-hill.

Small fish swam by, their characteristics struck Jack as weird. The front half of them was white while black on the back half. It was as if someone drew a straight line down the middle and painted them. They were cool. Jack watched them swim around for a while, as they swam by his feet. One of them nibbled at his big toe causing him to jerk his foot and they quickly scattered away.

Jack swam over to the edge of the pond where a tree had roots into the water. The roots were thick and formed a circle-like shape. He noticed something strange rippling below him and swam down to take a closer look. It was a light, and it came out of what looked like a small tunnel. His lungs began to hurt so he surfaced, took a large gulp of air and went back down, half expecting the tunnel to disappear, but the light was still there. It didn't appear to be very long and he was very curious as to where it led.

Jack surfaced to take another breath of air, holding on to the thick tree roots that now clearly seemed to form a doorway below the water. *Should he do it? Could he make it to the other end?* He couldn't resist the temptation; he had to give it a try. Jack looked around the area, mustering up his courage, his stomach felt like it was quivering, and then he took as deep a breath as he could and pulled himself back down using the roots. He held on to the roots for a second or two. There was barely enough space for him to get through, and his heart pounded against his chest with excitement. It couldn't be far. It didn't look like it was far. He could see end of the tunnel, maybe fifteen or twenty yards. He was sure he could make that.

Just do it you chicken! his mind screamed. "Your air is going to run out!" came his own inner retort.

He thrust onward, using the slippery muddy sides to help pull himself through as fast as humanly possible, the water turning cloudy behind him. There was no turning back now. There wasn't enough room to turn around and besides, he was at least half way. Jack began having second thoughts about this. It was farther than he thought and his lungs were now screaming for air.

This was a bad idea, Jack! You're going to die in this tunnel and no one will know you're here. You'll just disappear off the face of the Earth. His mind raced with thoughts of his parents, his friends, his school, as he struggled feverishly to reach the end.

Jack pulled and pulled as fast and as hard as he could. Just as his lungs were about to burst and he thought he surely wasn't going to make it, that he was going to drown right then and there, Jack jettisoned out of the hole into the open water. He kicked his feet and pulled at the water wildly until his head broke through the surface.

Jack took a heavy breath, grabbing the closest thing to hold on to. He sighed with relief while suddenly noticing the temperature difference of the water. It wasn't cold, but it wasn't hot as before, either. Looking at what he was holding on to, a large tree root came into focus. Just like on the other side of the tunnel, there, on the bank of the pond above the tunnel, was a large tree whose roots reached into the water and cradled the tunnel he had just came out of. Jack smiled at his success; then sighed with relief at his stupidity.

"You could have died, you idiot!" He didn't know if he wanted to cry or laugh.

"Cool," he said after he had a moment to collect himself, then he laughed out loud. He began to look around.

It was another pond about the same size and shape as his. "Weird," Jack thought. He had never noticed another pond, especially this close to his. Surely he would have seen it. If this tunnel connected the two ponds, how could he have missed it? The water was definitely colder here, like the public pools, and there was no burnt match smell, either and the water was crystal clear. *How could there be such a difference between two connected bodies of water?* Jack tossed these thoughts around in his head until he began to tire of treading water for he had drifted out towards the center of this new pond.

Jack made his way to the side of the pond and climbed out of the water using a tree root and searched around the area some more. The trees seemed to be a lot taller and the leaves were different. He looked up and it looked like he was looking through a telescope at the sky; it was definitely bluer than it was just a few minutes earlier. His mind flashed back to the water and he noticed the bottom wasn't muddy around the sides, either. It was rocky which had made it kind of hard on his feet climbing out. Ah! and where was the other pond?

He sat on the ground to rest a few minutes and think, he was so confused. It was so quiet. There was no wind and the air felt cooler. A chill made him shudder. *It's probably the air on my wet skin,* Jack told himself. He got up and walked around the pond, noticing that there were a lot more trees, thicker and closer together. Where was the big log? His clothes? The backpack? *Surely, there is a way to walk around to the other pond,* Jack reassured himself, *There just has to be a logical explanation for all this.* He felt so out of place all of the sudden, like something wasn't right. Where was *his* pond? It should be right there. Jack pointed to where he thought it should be as if he were showing himself. He turned around and around slowly. The woods were certainly denser.

He looked back into the pond. Maybe he better just swim back through the tunnel, back to his side. He walked around to the large tree with the large roots that crawled into the water like Boa Constrictor. The light wasn't there anymore. And neither was the tunnel. Fear began to settle into his stomach.

Jack walked maybe fifty yards towards what he thought was the direction he had come, but nothing was familiar. He returned and then went another fifty yards in a different direction. Jack did this in the four different directions, north, south, east, and west, without finding anything familiar. He began feeling really bad about this. It just didn't seem to be the same woods he was in earlier today. He went back into the water and checked for the tunnel again, to be sure, so he could swim back to his pond, but when he got to the spot, his fears were confirmed, the light and the tunnel were gone.

He began to panic. Jack returned to the water and swam the entire perimeter of the pond under water, looking desperately for the tunnel, but it just wasn't to be found. There was no fog in this water, it was crystal clear. It was the same tree with the large trunk that went into the water s but the underwater passageway had just disappeared. No light—No tunnel.

He climbed back out of the water, fighting the fear that was rapidly taking control over him. The woods were growing darker. He kept exploring, desperately looking for something familiar. His feet were sore now from stepping on twigs he didn't notice. Jack, exhausted from his search, overwhelmed with hopelessness, finally sank to his knees, clenched his hands in front of him and lowered his head. He was totally and utterly lost – and beginning to feel very cold.

God, my parents, he thought. He was going to be in some really serious trouble if he wasn't there for supper. "Ha, ha," he laughed nervously shaking his head, "as if I'm not now."

He looked up through watery eyes that blurred his vision, but could see through the trees that it would be dark in a couple of hours. Painfully, like an old tired man, he pulled himself up to his feet. *Which way should I go?* Jack thought as he began to shiver. He had no clothes, no money, and was now hungry and tired. Worry set in. Home began to look really good to him right about now. He began to look for shelter, but then thought, *maybe I'll run into someone for help. Yes, that's it, Sherlock. Find some help. Stop feeling sorry for yourself and do something. That was what his grandpa always told him when he complained about something.*

Jack happened upon a cluster of branches with numerous leaves that formed somewhat of a cave a short distance away that seemed to invite him to rest. Suddenly feeling tired, he opted to crawl under them and laid his head on his arm. The leaves blocked the gentle wind and their perfume of pine and dirt drugged him into a slumber, or maybe it was just the exhaustion that overcame him. Jack slept as Mother Nature turned off her lights and said goodnight.

CHAPTER 4

My New World

New is often scary
Full of challenges and tests
Making one most wary
Yet bringing out one's talents and their best

The birds awoke him with a softness that was much more pleasant than that of the alarm clock in his room. Jack yawned and stretched in his leafy bed and opened his sleepy eyes, the thoughts of his predicament a million miles away until the chill of the morning cleared the fog in his head. He sat up quickly, unpleasantly smacking leaves around his head, and looked at his surroundings, heart beating fast, still somewhat dazed from the slumber. Then, little by little, like taking small sips of water, reality forced its way in, reminding Jack of how he came to be sleeping in the woods.

Jack crawled out from under the branches, stood up and stretched out the stiffness from sleeping on the hard ground. The air felt brisk and he could tell that daylight had just begun. He did some body twists to loosen up, but actually felt well rested, despite the sleeping conditions and rapid heartbeat. He let out a deep sigh as his eyes scanned the area and his mind struggled to absorb his new surroundings.

Being lost didn't seem near so disastrous in the daylight. Or did he simply dream being lost? Jack wondered what his parents were doing. No doubt they called the police when he didn't show up for dinner or return to the house last night. They had no idea where he was and neither did he. Right now, his parents yelling at him for not coming home didn't seem like so much trouble. Jack decided to return to the pond and see if he could find his way back.

Okay, Jack. Just like you did with Dad-years ago-on those camping trips, hiking through the woods, re-member? One step at a time, Dad always said: 'KISS, KISS', Keep It Simple Stupid, he thought.

Finding the pond was no trouble, he really hadn't gone but several yards sleeping quite near it. But, when he looked by the tree and scanned the entire area, there still was no light, no tunnel, the water was still cool, and the bottom was still rocky. This was definitely not his pond. The trees were huge by comparison. His tree trunk seat was not there and neither was his backpack and clothes.

"These are not your woods, Jack! You gotta find help, dude," he said out loud to himself. He began making his way through the forest while looking back every few steps.

Jack suddenly stopped and turned around. *How will I find my way back to the pond?* It was as if he could get lost in a world he was already lost in. Confusion started creeping into Jack's mind, something was squeezing his brain, and his stomach was tied into a knot.

Why didn't I bring Red along? No, Red would be the one to get me into these kinds of situations. This time I did it all by myself – and I'm going to get myself out of it, too. Think, Jack! he thought, smacking the heel of his open hand to his forehead.

He broke a branch off a tree and tore off its leaves, then other branches until he had made a stick man with two arms. He planted his creation in the ground making sure one arm was longer than the other to point towards the pond. He broke off several other branches and made about ten more similar stick men to mark his trail. He took a look back at his work as he continued on his way and felt brilliant. *This Robinson Crusoe stuff wasn't that hard.* As long as he didn't have to be Rambo, lighting gunpowder in a bullet wound and stuff like that, he'd be all right. A sense of excitement began to fill his chest. Jack had never been lost before, not *really* lost anyway. It was sort of like an adventure—a scary one. He took a deep breath and sighed, looking ahead. He just hoped this adventure wouldn't be a permanent one. *"Think positive,"* Jack, he thought.

He traveled some time, maybe an hour or so, noticing that it took longer walking through the woods barefoot hearing the many ooches and ouches that burst from within him, at what seemed like every other step, before he happened onto a small cave. Jack picked up a rock and threw it with all his strength into the cave. If something came out he'd run. But then the thought flashed through his mind that he wouldn't be able to outrun any animal in bare feet. Too late— Jack's stomach tightened. He heard the rock hit and bounce on the walls, the clatter hushing the birds nearby, and then full silence. He was crouched and ready to run for his life if anything came out of there. Barefoot or not, a bear or any other large creature would make him forget about having no shoes.

Jack listened, no animals came running out. The birds, began their chorus once again. The sun was getting high enough now to send its rays of light and warmth through the thick conglomerate of woods and the warmth penetrated his chilled body and the thick forest blocked most of the wind for which he was glad. The sunlight shone dimly to the back wall of stone. He cautiously entered the cave. The floor was of dirt and stone while the sides were rock, also. It didn't go back far, maybe ten feet, but then there was a small opening in the wall to the right, as if it were cut out;

just big enough for him to lie down in. Jack remembered his Sunday school classes and the picture the pastor had showed them of Jesus' cave where he rose from the dead. His pastor also told him God was always watching over him, well he could sure use His help right now. This would make a good shelter for the night, much better than last night anyway.   His stomach was tying itself into knots and his throat felt dry. Drinking water was a priority, food was right beneath it. Jack piled a bunch of stones at the entrance and made a few more stick men. At least his shorts were dry. The idea of rain drove a sigh to his lips—that's all he needed, just like in the movies where everything goes wrong for the good guy and then, on top of it all, it starts raining. Fortunately, it didn't look like rain as Jack looked up through the pine trees at the spots of clear blue sky.

Jack had gone another hour's walk and began to wonder if he'd ever find help, a town or anything at this point. He wondered how long it was going to be before he found some kind of civilization. Maybe he should have walked in the opposite direction. He saw no choice but to keep on going, still marking the trail.

The unmistakable sound of leaves cracking kept popping close enough to Jack making the hair on his arms stand. He looked around him and quickened his pace. The birds had stopped singing and silence hung heavy in the woods. *"That's not good,"* Jack thought nervously.

He turned around slowly and looked behind him. Above the cave he had just left minutes ago, tress were swaying as if yanked to catapult something. His heart raced as he turned and began running through the trees as fast as he could, not feeling his feet breaking the twigs or stepping on the pine needles.

He had seen nothing really, yet he flew like the wind, left and right, through the trees, knowing he couldn't really outrun a wild animal, but the lingering pang of panic overreaction hung over him. Had he just wigged over nothing? He seemed to be running a long distance when he had to stop suddenly. There was a deep ravine with a river. He couldn't jump across, it was too wide. He turned and listened.

Jack looked left and right and noticed a fallen tree across the ravine. He quickly made his way to the tree and began to cross. He stopped halfway as the tree began to move and give. This was an old trunk and certainly made him aware that it wouldn't hold much longer. The river screamed below. Unsure of whether he heard any noise behind him or the shear panic sound coming from his mind, he resolved to continue, the choice was made for him and staying on that side was not it. He continued more slowly until he finally got to the other side and jumped to safety.

The pain from his bleeding bare feet gnawed at his whole body. He turned and looked back across to see a mountain lion just beginning to cross over the same tree trunk. He froze. *"Do something, Jack!"* his mind screamed, but the cat was agile and effortlessly making his way towards him—already halfway across before he could move. Jack grabbed one of the branches holding the tree on his side of the ravine and lifted with all his strength, a strength a human has only in times of a great emergency. The tree shifted and the branch broke. Jack fell towards the ravine, slipped and tumbled barely able to catch himself at the edge, his legs hanging off the edge. A piercing shriek followed as the trunk fell—too close for comfort, carrying the mountain lion with him. Jack's vision blurred and his grip loosened as heat seared across his back, pushing a scream as the breath was knocked out of him.

He clasped harder and regained his grip perilously, instinctively knowing it would be short-lived. The waves of pain sheeting from his back were stealing all the strength he had left. This is where his life would end, he thought. His breathing was shallow and rapid, his hands were slipping once more and his mind was racing. Jack closed his eyes, took in a painful breath and with a deep cry he pulled himself up. Falling on the ground face forward. Relief and excruciating agony coursed through him.

For some time, Jack was unable to move, catching his breath and muttering through the burn in his back. He guessed that the tree trunk had grazed and if the mountain lion emerged he was dead, he had no strength to outrun him and he didn't know if he had died on the fall. Jack forced himself to stand up and looked back. His back was wet, he reached to check, gasping and recoiling at the motion. Blood was oozing, thick and substantial. This was serious. The tree had fallen and crashed below into the river. It was wedged across the river, the water hitting it and spilling over. He frantically searched for the cat amidst his pain. When he couldn't spot it, he turned and expected to see it right behind him, but it wasn't there, either. Jack kneeled and watched the river for a good five minutes before he felt confident he had escaped death. He took a deep breath "I have to move. If there was one, were there more?" His words ached over his dry throat.

He forced himself to stand, but sat back down quickly. He looked at the bottom of his feet. He pulled out several pine needles and noticed he was still bleeding on both feet. His head dropped in hopelessness, but he mustered up his strength and got to his feet. Jack pushed on, walking on the outsides of his feet. His eyes watered with the pain, his breathing was increasingly laboring, but his bit his lip and continued.

Jack stopped to rest a moment and remembered when he and his Grandpa had gone camping a couple of years back. His Grandpa had fallen and gashed his leg pretty bad, but he kept walking until he could return to camp. He could see his face, full of pain, but he also saw the determination, defying the pain. He looked down at his feet, then looked straight ahead and tightened his jaw, nodded his head, and began to walk.

Through shaky hands he precariously made some more stick men to mark his way. Hopelessness was gaining on him once again as he placed the last of the five additional stick men in the ground. Jack turned and looked around to find more twigs from which to make more.

Then, right there in front of him, Jack couldn't believe it, he was finally blessed with a stroke of luck. He looked up into the sky with jubilation and said, "Thank you." There, down on the bottom of an incline, was a small wooden cabin. He could forget the cave now.

He began to walk towards the cabin, but then stopped suddenly.

"Not so fast, Jack," he said softly to himself. Last bit of conscious sense tugging at him, through a hazy and drowsy feeling.

He didn't know who would be there. Jack looked all around the area for at least a couple of minutes forcing a squatting position, remaining as silent as possible. Rambo's movie coming into memory, he touched his right hip. Nope, no knife. He was sure he was delirious. Was he losing more blood than he could tell? The back of his shorts felt wet from the blood. The sound of birds snapped him back to reality. He remembered his Dad's words, telling him something when they had gone camping.

As long as the birds are singing and the crickets are chirping, everything's okay. His dad was a veteran of some war, a Marine, "Semper Fi," he always said. He learned a lot about camping from his Dad.

He decided to approach cautiously and waited behind some bushes where he could see the cabin from about fifty yards away. Jack waited for a good thirty minutes, or what seemed like thirty minutes, considering there was no real way to tell in the present conditions. It was probably only five or ten. He kept expecting to see someone come out of the cabin or go by the window or something, not really knowing why he thought that. Maybe he was just scared. There weren't any cars, or motorcycles, or even bicycles parked in front of the cabin and he couldn't see any likes of them for as far the eye could reach, which wasn't very far in the thick woods.

That's strange, he thought to himself as he just realized there wasn't even a road leading to the cabin or anywhere in sight. Not even a worn path.

When he was confident no one was moving about, he summoned up the courage and sneaked up to the front door and knocked. He took a couple of steps back and waited, legs trembling slightly, hoping to be able to run like a deer, well, a hobbled one, if need be. Jack glanced behind and then to each side of himself several times. There was no answer. He knocked again with more confidence, louder this time. The quiver in his knees subsided and his heartbeat began to slow down.

Still, there was no answer. He turned the door handle, but it didn't budge. The wood of the cabin was in bad need of paint, he thought. The more he observed the more the place actually looked abandoned. Jack went to a window and looked inside. There was a simple square wooden table with four rustic wooden chairs. Along the right wall was a fireplace. On the left, Jack spotted two doors that he assumed led to other rooms.

He tried pushing the window up and surprisingly it moved. Jack smiled in relief, raised it high as it would open and climbed inside. He stood and looked around, admitting to himself, this was a little exciting just a little. He left the window open, just in case he had to make a run for it.

"Hello? Anybody home?" Jack tried to yell out, but his voice came out broken up and soft, almost like a loud hoarse whisper.

There was no answer.

"Anyone home?" He yelled again, after clearing his throat as loud as he could. This time his voice came out loud and clear and he scared himself a little at its reverberation, for the sound echoed slightly in the barren room. He glanced behind and around himself, then looked out the window, just in case there was someone in the woods close by.

There was still no answer. The floor was made of wood so it wasn't cold on his feet. Its smooth surface gave respite to the cutup skin on the bottom of his feet.

He went over to the first of the doors and gingerly pushed it open. It led to a bathroom that reminded Jack of the old John Wayne movies he watched occasionally with Grandpa. There was a small white plastic seat on top of a wooden box on the right and a white PVC tube extended through the wood and up through the ceiling. A half roll of toilet paper rested beside the toilet seat. "A toilet!" Jack yipped. On the left side of the room Jack spotted a large oval galvanized metal tub, like the cowboys used to bathe in. Between the tub and the toilet, hung a small white enamel sink with rusted faucets. "Probably don't work." Said Jack. There were brown rust stains on the enamel from the keys drawing a path to a drain, which seemed to be connected to the box of the commode.

Jack relieved himself, glad he didn't have to worry about flushing. The hole in the wood was so deep he couldn't see the bottom. Jack didn't want to leave any evidence that he was here, and, from the looks of it, it probably wouldn't have worked anyway, from lack of use.

Jack made his way into the other room, finding a thin mattress laid on top of a box of wood constructed to its size. It wasn't attractive like his bed at home, but it looked more inviting to him than the cave. The only other furniture was a large, dark brown wooden trunk at the foot of the bed that looked too heavy for some-one to carry.

Jack looked inside it. The lid was really heavy, at least in his weakened state it was. There were a couple of heavy wool looking blankets, one pink and another light blue. Two small pillows lay on top of the blankets covered with pink pillow cases. Everything looked clean.

Why so much pink? flashed through Jack's mind, but just for a second. There were more important things to attend to.

Confident he was alone; Jack went back to the kitchen and found some canned foods on a single shelf attached to the wall. He lacked energy and could tell he was still bleeding from his back. The pain was a constant reminder. He grabbed a can of Vienna sausages and a can of baked beans. His mouth watered with anticipation and his stomach began to churn so violently he felt he may vomit before having a chance to eat. He hurried in his task.

Scouring around produced a hand operated can opener for the baked beans, the Vienna sausages had a pop-top lid. some metal forks, knives, spoons, and some plastic ones in a tray left on a shelf under the sink. There were no doors to hide any shelves any-where. "Practical," said Jack. You could see where everything's at without having to open doors, like you do at home.

He grabbed a spoon and pretentiously wiped it clean on his shorts. Then Jack went to the kitchen table and sat, grimacing over the speed with which he descended on the heavy wooden chair that faced the door. "I see you," said Jack to it, "stay shut." He placed the two cans and the spoon in front of him, then pried off the lid of the beans and pulled the tab on the Vienna sausages. Taking a spoon, Jack dug into the beans with a fleeting vengeance, while also pulling the sausages out with his fingers. He thought he swallowed the first two whole, they were so small.

Jack was so hungry he didn't taste much of the food. It was more like he inhaled both cans of grub so fast it felt as if the food got stuck half way down his throat. He waited with discomfort until he felt the lump go away, noticing how good it tasted.

He then found some bottles of water under the sink area and opened one. It was empty within seconds, cooling his hoarse, dry throat. Jack stood by the sink, breathing heavily, letting his stomach handle what he just shoved and poured down his throat.

At least he had a bed for now. He relaxed and took his time now walking around the cabin inside and out. The food supply wouldn't last more than a day or two, unless he really stretched it out. Maybe he could find some fruits or nuts somewhere close by. "What am I going to do?" he asked himself. There were three of the gallon bottles of water on a shelf and another opened bottle was on the floor below them. "At least water is not a problem." Jack sighed.

Jack found a glass and wiped it out with a paper towel. He poured and downed two more glasses of water, it felt good. Getting lost was a really thirsty business.

He was desperately tired and sleepy, so he took the blue blanket and a pillow out of the trunk and carefully laid on his side on the bed. The warmth of the blanket felt really good and the pillow was nice and soft.

Just an hour, Jack thought. Then he would continue the search for civilization. At least for now, he had a decent place to stay. *First things first, Dad, right?* His eyelids became lead weights and he drifted off into his dream world.

CHAPTER 5

California

Here I was, in a void of space
Finally to find its location
Narrowly escaping the police by race
Still not knowing how to solve my situation

Jack awakened with a start. He wondered where in the world he was as he looked all around the room; and then everything came back to him like a wave of water. He had no idea what time it was except that it was still daytime, because of the light that came through the window. And now it just dawned on him, he hadn't noticed any clocks in the cabin.

He wondered if someone found his stuff back at his pond. His cell phone and his tablet were in his backpack. *Please God, keep them for me. If someone stole those, I don't think I could ever go home. It'd be sui-cide.* Jack thought.

He got up and went outside. The sun was still pretty high so he guessed it was probably around one or two in the afternoon. Jack sat on the porch step of the little wooden cabin and held his head inside his hands.

"What am I going to do? Here I am in a place I've never been, no clothes— wait, there was that trunk..."

He jumped to his feet, almost tripped running back into the bedroom, wincing over the pain on his back he threw open the trunk, digging under the blankets. He smiled as he pulled out a grey t-shirt that read 49ers, Super Bowl Champions 2016. "2016?"

"Someone really screwed up. May be worth some bucks, though," he said. *Somebody had it made, for sure. That's it. The NFL would never make a mistake like that and let it get out of the factory.* He shrugged his shoulders and slipped it over his head, cringing as it slid over the wound that was ever so present, though he could not really see it. Jack felt some relief however, as he considered that the pain had lessened and there was no more blood running down his back. "Not my team, but it'll work." He noted the gray shirt matched his shorts except his shorts had black lettering and the shirt had red. There were no shoes, but he found a pair of flip-flops in the bathroom by the tub that would help. He didn't care for them being pink, but after all, "beggars can't be choosers," as his Dad would say, and he couldn't be too choosy right now. They seemed to fit okay.

Hunger cried out from within again steering Jack back to the food shelf to see what he could find. *Hey, a can of spaghetti. That'll work.* He opened the can and looked around for a microwave. Then he remembered. No microwave. He grabbed the fork he had left on the table from 'breakfast' and cleaned it on his shorts, again. Jack used the can opener once again, and then sat down at the table to enjoy his lunch. He was expecting the cold spaghetti to taste terrible, but it actually tasted good. He nodded his approval as he continued.

What was he going to do now? He slurped down a mouthful of spaghetti, while pondering. There had to be a town around here somewhere. Jack sighed, hoping this wasn't one of those cabins, way up in the mountains some twenty miles away from any town. He finished his gourmet meal, drank two glasses of water, thinking he'd better store up on the precious liquid, and then headed back outdoors.

Jack made several more stick men to mark his trail before venturing off in search of help. The day was calm and the forest was peaceful. There were a lot of birds, some with yellow, and some with black markings. He heard the song of the cardinal, though he never saw one. As he made his way through the woods he kept a sharp ear and eye out for any more mountain lions, but the serenity of Mother Nature and the constant songs the birds sang to him kept him calm.

He finally came to the end of the woods and saw a street with a row of homes. Relief! There was a big grassy area that formed a rectangular barrier Jack imagined was put there to keep people out of the woods. He smiled. That wouldn't stop anyone he knew.

"And they say kids are so naïve," he chuckled to himself.

He stood at the edge of the woods behind one of the thick blue spruce trees and observed. The first house was made of boring beige wood. The front yard was very green and well kept. There were four more homes and the same number of homes on the opposite side of the street. The short street was lined with trees on both sides and he could see it turned only to the left at the end.

Really small neighborhood, he reasoned.

Jack was getting nervous. The first house had a black sedan style car in the driveway. *Someone should be home.* He meandered down to it and cautiously knocked on the door. It opened and a tall woman with thick glasses filled the doorway. He was torn between running and staying and crying. Not knowing if he was relieved or scared, Jack's feet were glued to the ground at present, so he stayed.

"Can I help you, young man?"

He was thankful she spoke English though he didn't know why he thought she would speak any other language, and that an actual person lived there. And it was an adult. Jack was extremely happy to see an adult. He would never have believed it. He blinked his eyes and stared. She wore a bright yellow plain blouse and a black pair of slacks.

"Hello? Can I help you?" She repeated.

"Oh. Hi. Sorry. I, uh…" Jack found he really didn't know how to begin. He searched for the words, his mouth hung open.

"Well? I haven't got all day, young man."

"Well, uh. Sorry. I, –um, I think I'm lost." The last part blurted out in a hurry.

"Lost?" She smiled and chuckled. She thought he was kidding.

"Where do you live, son?"

"Spring." *Oh, please, God, tell me that I am in Spring,* the thought came.

"Spring?" Never heard of it. Guess you are lost. How old are you?"

His heart sank heavily to his stomach. His mind struggled with the news.

"Fourteen," came out not much louder than a whisper. *Oh, here we go with all those grown-up questions.*

"What school do you go to?"

"Daley-Brammel," Jack answered pointing to his shorts bearing the school name on them.

She looked down at the shorts, making Jack feel uneasy about the blank look on her face.

"Daley-Brammel. Never heard of that school, either. Know your phone?"

"Yes, of course."

"Well, come in. Let's see if we can't find out where home is. Got any ID?"

"No. I..." He didn't want to tell her he had left it in his backpack on a tree trunk by a pond he seemed to have lost, also.

"I lost my wallet, too."

"Wow. You're really in a mess, aren't you? What's your name?"

"Jack. Jack West, ma'am."

She looked at him as if she didn't believe he gave her his real name. He got that a lot everywhere he went, though. It was like saying your name is John Doe. He remembered his first day in Daley-Brammel. Even the teachers asked him if Jack West was his real name, the one on his birth certificate-*As if he could give them any name he wanted*. He would get ribbed with many silly comments from the other students about whether he was from the West, from West Texas, or if he always wanted to go West.

She led Jack into the kitchen and motioned for him to sit down. She pulled a cold canned cola beverage out of the fridge and set it in front of him.

"Thanks!" Jack replied to the gift. Quickly opening it and downing about half the can, following it up with a loud burp from the gas.

"Sorry," Jack said, red-faced, filled with embarrassment.

"Thirsty, too, aren't you?" She chuckled and smiled as she pulled out her phone. "Hard to believe a boy fourteen years old is lost. Tell me your phone number, son."

"281-803-4495," Jack dictated.

He looked around the kitchen. It had the typical brown wooden cabinets. *All with doors*, he smiled at the thought, his mind flashing back to the cabin. He was sitting at a glass top kitchen table with four light brown wooden chairs, each with a dark green cushion on them. It smelled like flowers in the house and Jack didn't see any ashtrays around.

"281? Never heard of that area code, either." She went to a cabinet and pulled out a book that was like a miniature phone book and dropped it on the table with a thud. She kept glancing at Jack as if she suspected a prank or something. It made him nervous.

Jack felt a cold sweat come over as he read the cover of the phone book. "Wright Wood, California."

"What town is this?" He asked with a raspy voice.

"Wright Wood. Know it, don't you?" She was looking in the front pages at the listings for area codes and didn't look up at him.

"No, ma'am. I live in Texas." He almost whispered, his voice breaking.

"Texas! Why, my goodness, son! That's halfway across the country! How did you get here!?"

It made no sense. How could this be California? It wasn't possible, all he did was swim through a gap in a pond. Disbelief plagued over his dumbfounded expression. *Well, you see, ma'am, I swam through this tunnel in my pond and came out in California...no biggie.* Was the only thing that came to mind. That's what he wanted to say, but he really couldn't tell her that. She'd think he was crazy, not that she probably didn't already think that now. He searched for a lie but he just couldn't come up with one on such short notice. His friend Red was good at that.

"I…" Jack was at a loss for words, only being able to shake his head.

"Oh, my. (her face changed from suspicious to concern) Did you get hit on the head or something? Did somebody kidnap you and you escaped?" She began looking at his head, then body, for injuries. Concern filled the woman's voice and her face showed alarm.

"No, no. I. I just don't know. Really, ma'am. How am I going to get back?" He had really asked himself that question out loud.

"Don't worry, son. I'm sure your parents will figure out how. Let's call the number. What did you say it was?"

"281-803-4495." He was going to tell her they wouldn't be home, but then he remembered it was Sunday. They slept in late on Sundays, especially after being out the night before, then sometimes till one in the afternoon. If the lady woke them up, it would probably make them even angrier, but he was already in deep trouble, so...

"What are their names?"

"My Dad's name is Frank and my Mom's is Carol."

She nodded as she dialed. Then she pulled the phone away from her ear and looked at it strangely.

"You said 281-803-4495, right?"

"Yes, ma'am."

"The number you have dialed is not a working number or is no longer in service, please check the number and dial again," a recording announced in the woman's ear.

"Sure you got it right? You're not pulling my leg, here, right?" Her face changed from nice lady to 'you're in trouble'.

"No, honest." He began to think he made a really serious mistake coming here.

"Where did you get that shirt if you're from Texas?"

Oh, boy! She just went into full investigation mode.

"This? Oh, I found it. I didn't have a shirt to wear and..." Jack could see he was digging himself in deeper so he stopped.

"I think we better call the police to help you."

"Police?"

"Is that a problem? You in trouble with the law?"

"No, no. Never. Honest, ma'am."

The woman grabbed a small laptop that was on the kitchen counter and opened it on the kitchen table.

"Let's see here.   You said you lived in what, Spring, Texas, right?"

"Yes, ma'am." Jack desperately wanted to just run out of there.

"We'll see.   Well now.   Spring, Texas does exist. Houston area."

"Yes.   That's it." Jack let out a sigh and felt somewhat relieved that *something* came out right.

"Well.   We'll let the police get you home to Spring."   She called the police and stepped into the living room to explain Jack's 'problem' in private. Adults always want to talk about you in private.   That always got his dander up.

Jack got up and was just about to make a mad dash when he saw a newspaper lying on the kitchen counter. He read the date.

"Saturday, May 29, 2016."

His heart beat wildly and his mind felt it was going to explode.   He tippy-toed to the door, pulled off his shower shoes so he could move faster, then bolted out as fast as his legs could carry him, back through the grassy area that separated the houses from the woods and into the safety of the trees.

He followed the stickmen as fast as he could, picking them up after him as he went, all the way back to the cabin in the woods, closing the window behind him.   Jack sank into one of the kitchen chairs, out of breath, trying desperately to figure out what just happened. He looked out the window.

Was this a dream? If it was, he wanted desperately to wake up. Jack looked down at his shirt. 2016. The year he read was 2016! He shook his head. It was supposed to be 2014! Was this a Rip Van Winkle story?

He had to find a way back home by himself. The sun was on its way down. The pond was a couple of hours away and he wouldn't be able to do much in the dark. The only way home had to be the pond. He would have to check it again tomorrow, leave early in the morning so he would have plenty of time to return to the cabin if things didn't pan out. The mountain lion popped up in the back of his mind. The wound throbbed. He closed his eyes and took a deep breath.

Maybe you have gone crazy, Jack.

He sat at the table with his head over his arms resting on the table. Right now Jack thought he'd rather have his parents yelling at him for not coming home and losing his tablet and cell phone and whatever.

"I promise, Lord. I'll do what you say. Respect my Mother and father. I'll even try to do things to help them. Just let me get home," he said with all sincerity to God, looking up at the wooden ceiling.

He got up, poured himself a glass of water, and sat pondering, felling very sorry for himself. He couldn't call a single friend in the neighborhood to help him out. He couldn't even call an aunt or uncle, or grandma or grandpa. He couldn't even call someone he hated. He was all alone. Dropping his head in his hands again, a single tear of frustration rolled down his right cheek and Jack wiped it away, angry with himself for being weak and stupid.

He remembered what the minister had told them in Sunday School.

"Remember, God is always with you. When in need of help, just ask. He'll be there for you and with you."

"Well. I'm asking now." He looked up and shook his head. "Help?" He said softly.

Jack hoped God heard whispers.

CHAPTER 6

More Complications

Girls are people too
Who have different things to do
Others try to make them become
Someone other than their hearts do drum

Meagan returned home to find only her brother present. She hurried to her room and carefully placed the specimen in a plastic container. She anchored a piece of plastic on top with a rubber band and then punched some holes in it for air.

Because she was home, Meagan decided to have lunch. She ate a ham and cheese sandwich and a bag of chips and then started for the door.

"Where are you going?" asked her little brother.

"To Amber's." Came a fleeting answer as the door shut behind Meagan.

When Susan, Meagan's mother, returned home from her food shopping duties around four, which included a stop at the local mall, she called out for Meagan to help put the food away.

"She said something about going to Amber's house, Mom." Tyler was Meagan's ten year old, younger brother. Meagan looked like her Mother while Tyler looked just like his Dad with dark, curly brown hair and hazel eyes whose irises were speckled with yellow tiny dots.

"When did she tell you this?" His Mom, questioned as she walked into the kitchen. Tyler sat at the kitchen table spreading grape jelly over the peanut butter he had just finished spreading on two pieces of whole wheat bread.

"Couple of hours ago. She came home for lunch." He assembled his creation and immediately sampled it.

"She didn't tell me she was going to Amber's house," she said, more to herself than to Tyler.

"It's Saturday," was Tyler's response, as if it explained Meagan's disappearance naturally.

Susan nodded her understanding. Meagan wasn't one to hang around the house like Tyler. Tyler could spend all day at home on the Xbox, but Meagan was different. She loved the outdoors. She was an early riser and wanted to be outside when the sun broke the horizon. She shuddered at the thought of all those in-sects she kept in her room.

"Lunch time was more than a couple of hours ago, Tyler. I wanted her to help me clean the bathrooms. She'll just have to give up her Sunday afternoon, then." Once again, talking to herself more than to Tyler.

"We gonna have to go to church, Mom?"

"Of course we *have* to go to church! Don't we always go every Sunday?"

"Aw, Mom. Baseball. Dad and I want to watch the games."

"You and your father can watch your baseball after we get back from church, as always."

"Aw, man. We'll miss the first half of the first game."

"Well that's just too bad, young man. God is first."

Tyler noted her tone was akin to a reprimand so he just pouted and turned his attention back to his peanut butter and jelly sandwich.

"I want *you* to clean up your room before you go anywhere, hear?"

"Aw, Mom," he complained with a full mouth.

"Don't 'aw' me. And don't talk with food in your mouth. Mind your manners. Now come help me put the food away."

"Yes, Ma'am," Tyler said resignedly and slid off the kitchen chair and began helping his Mother, carrying his sandwich with him and regretting he hadn't snuck off to his room before the conversation had even started.

Meagan never stayed home on the weekends if she wasn't forced to. She was one of those 'tomboys'. She joined her Dad and brother when it came to the 49ers and jumped and shouted during the games as much or more than Tyler. Susan always felt sort of like an outsider on Sundays during football season. She had always thought football was stupid. Grown men intentionally hitting each other as hard as they could. In Susan's mind, men never grew up. Although she hoped her daughter would eventually grow out of it, Susan knew Meagan loved sports as much, if not more than Theodore, her husband, did. Meagan was a good soccer player at school, also.

She got straight A's in school while Tyler just barely got by with C's. Susan tried frequently to get Meagan to play an instrument or take ballet lessons, but Meagan refused and Theodore simply said, "why waste money on something she doesn't want to do?" Her husband was just fine with her playing soccer and attempted to make it to every one of her games.

Susan wanted her husband to work more with Tyler to get his grades up but Theodore just waved the point off.

"Relax, Dear. He'll come around when he's ready," Theodore would say when she showed him Tyler's report card every six weeks. It was always the same discussion. Theodore was a civil engineer and never achieved good grades when he was in school, nor when he played football at Southern Cal. "Tyler will be just fine. Just give 'im his space," he would say.

Meagan was relieved her Mother wasn't home, enabling her to escape the house and her Mother's constant chores. Hurrying for the edge of the woods after gulping down her sandwich and stuffing more food in her backpack, Meagan slowed her walk to a crawl as she passed her aunt's house. There were two police cars and another car with Social Services written on the door in front of her aunt's house, but the emergency lights weren't flashing.

Looks like someone's in trouble. There were no officers outside. *Hope it's not serious.* Curiosity made her want to stop and see what was going on, but she felt very uncomfortable around police officers, even though her uncle was one. Besides, Meagan didn't want to delay getting to her secret place any longer, so she continued into the woods, looked back down the street one last time and then blended into the sanctum of the woods.

It seemed funny to her that there were no other people on the street. Her aunt had probably just invited the policemen over for lunch as an excuse to discuss something in the neighborhood. She smiled at the thought and shook her head. Meagan's aunt liked to meddle in everyone else's business. Her Mother didn't really care much for the woman. Meagan shrugged her shoulders, pulled a phone out of her jeans pocket and pressed Amber from the contacts list.

"Hi Meagan. What's up?"

"Hi Am. Listen. Do me a favor. If Mom calls, tell her I'm with you, okay?"

"I'm not going to be here. I'm going to Lucy's house."

"Perfect. Tell your Mom I'm supposed to go there, too. Tell her you're meeting me and we're going over there together. That way, when Mom calls later, your Mom will cover for me."

"You're gonna get me in trouble again, Meagan, aren't you?"

"No, no, I'm not. If it comes up later, just tell your Mother I never showed up, that's all."

"So where you going this time, anyway?"

"Just in the woods. Bug searching. You know."

"Yuck! Why in the world do you like playing with those gross bugs and stuff?"

"I just think they're interesting. That's all."

"Why don't you just tell your Mom you're looking at bugs?"

"'Cause she wants me to dance ballet and play the piano or violin. You know, girlie stuff. I don't like that, it's boring. If I told her I was going to look at insects, she'd have a fit and keep me at home. Besides, she always thinks of some chores for me to do.

She wants me to do her job. The house is like a jail when you can't get out."

"I dance ballet and I don't think it's boring. It's classical."

"You're just repeating what the adults say. It's classical. Ha! Whoop ti do. Looking at yourself in the mirror stretching your legs all out of shape and stuff."

"Well, you get to wear all those really nice outfits and travel to different cities to perform. That's not boring!"

"To me it is. I don't like wearing those tights and dresses. They look terribly uncomfortable. Besides, I would look ridiculous. It's just not me, Am, and you know it. The traveling's okay, though, if you could do what you want, that is. So. Gonna cover for me, Am, right?"

"Yeah, okay, Meg. I'm leaving in a couple of minutes, anyway. And if Mom doesn't ask, I'm not saying anything."

"Perfect. See ya tomorrow in church. And thanks."

Meagan smiled to herself and continued walking casually through the woods towards her secret spot. She inhaled deeply the scent of leaves and looked up through the trees into the pale blue sky. The sun would go down in a couple of hours. She still had plenty of time to get there. Whenever Meagan entered her world she felt surrounded by peace and tranquility. Here it seemed the world just flowed like a peaceful stream somehow. It was as if every animal, every insect, even the air, was one living thing that seemed to be in perfect harmony and breathed in unison.

In these woods was where Meagan was happiest. She loved listening to the birds singing; watching the abundant variety of insects busily going about their lives, not caring what others did, but only concentrating on their task at hand. The bugs didn't meddle in other insect's business like humans were prone to do. Everyone did their job, nothing more, nothing less.

Green was Meagan's favorite color because her world was bathed in it. She wasn't a fanatic about her color, like some of her friends were with their pink or purple, of which she preferred pink, purple was so ugly, but she believed green made her feel more natural. Her Mother always bought her pink things; constantly telling her to be more feminine. Maybe she'd start being more feminine when she was older, but for now, it was way too much trouble.

Her destination was only about twenty minutes ahead of her. She cheerfully and casually strolled through her world, unaware that she was on a collision course.

CHAPTER 7

Surprise

A friend in need is a friend indeed
But can I give my trust to her?
Sometimes a planted seed becomes a weed
But sometimes it turns out to be a flower

Jack was immensely enjoying another can of spaghetti he had opened, even cold was becoming more and more tasty, when he heard a noise at the front door, like a key in a lock, and his heart raced as it suddenly burst open. Jack's mouth hung open, frozen in place, as did his hand holding the fork of soft noodles. The figure standing in the doorway also seemed to be in still animation.

This person had long straight blonde hair that hung down to her shoulders. Her face looked ghostly white with blue eyes that resembled two large round buttons. She stood frigid with her legs apart, her left hand on the doorknob, and her right hand hung in the air with a key held tightly between her thumb and forefinger.

"Who are you?" She demanded recovering from her shock before Jack.

Jack was caught red-handed, 'manos en la masa', as one of his Spanish friends always said.

"I. Uh.." Jack searched for words while his eyes scanned the room for a place to escape. No back door to this place. His face felt as if it was on fire and a tremendous wave of guilt fell over him.

"Well?" She stood waiting, her hands now on her waist, reminding Jack of his Mother's stance when she scolded him. She didn't seem to be in the least bit afraid.

"I knocked," were the only words Jack could find at the moment. The words were barely audible sounding scratchy and soft, sounding pretty lame.

"And no one answered so you came in and stole my food and water. You're a thief! Get out!" She took a few steps into the kitchen area and pointed to the door she had left wide open, giving her unwanted guest plenty of space to race to his freedom.

Jack glanced down at the almost empty can of spaghetti, still on the table in front of him along with a half glass of water.

"Sorry. I was hungry, and lost." Jack shrugged his shoulders and held up his hands, palms up, in resignation. He really wanted to get up and run out the door as she commanded, but he couldn't get his legs to move, he was glued in the chair with his hands up like someone under arrest.

She seemed to stare at him, thinking for a moment.

"Well, who are you then? And what are you doing here?" She suddenly seemed to take on such a calm air, walked over, and closed the door behind her. Meagan then bravely stepped forward in front of Jack on the opposite side of the table, as if he weren't any kind of threat to her at all. Jack didn't know if that was good or bad, but it certainly made him extremely nervous.

Meagan wore a white t-shirt that read Rock 'N Roll across the front with guitars all over it. Her jeans were well faded and hugged her legs.

"Jack West. That's my name." Rolling out of his mouth more like a burp rather than spoken. Boy, was he sounding dumb! *Jeez, you're really taking control of this situation, Jack!* His mind still felt jumbled, like everything was out of place inside.

"I'll leave. Don't worry. I just needed a place to crash until I find my way back. I'm, uh, really sorry. Really. I, uh, thought the place was abandoned. Really." Jack felt absolutely stupid for using 'really' so much but was finally getting his composure back, and his nerve. The cave flashed into his mind as a place to go, but so did the mountain lion..

Meagan sat down in the chair opposite from Jack. Jack's eyes got big and he slid back into his chair, not knowing what to expect next from this bold girl in front of him; that now leaned forward towards him on her forearms, staring with eyes he could feel go right through him. He had never met anyone like her before. Most girls Jack knew tried to tell everyone what to do and were very dominant in character, but this one seemed to challenge him, also. She was somehow, totally different, so confident, seemed quite intelligent for a reason he didn't understand, and was really pretty, especially her eyes.

"Jack West. Yeah. Sure. And I'm Shirley Temple. You're lost, huh? Like, really lost?" She cocked her head slightly to the right and her eyes told him she didn't believe him.

Jack stared at her wrapped in the vision her eyes, and then he shook his head slightly as if awakening. *Why am I thinking that at a time like this?* He displayed a weak smile.

"Yeah. I get that all the time. Yes, it's really Jack West. And it's kind of hard to explain how I'm lost, though. You'd never believe me anyway. I still don't believe it." Jack shook his head and lowered his eyes to the table with the incriminating evidence in front of him. He had never thrown away the other empty cans of sausages, beans and spaghetti he had eaten earlier, and the empty bottle of water lay beside them. It appeared as if he had really pigged out on her food. He finally put the fork full of spaghetti back into the can and released his hold on the utensil. Jack's palms were sweaty so he wiped them dry on his shorts.

"My name's Meagan. This is my cabin." She beat her finger into the middle of her chest a couple of times to emphasize the fact "My parents don't even know about it, either." she blundered.

"Really?" Jack thought about her words for a few seconds, then he smiled.

"Well, then. If your parent's don't know about this place, then it's really not your cabin, is it? You found it. Just like I did." For some reason Jack began feeling braver. A challenging grin filled his face.

"Yeah. Okay. You're right. But I found it first, a long time ago. Finders keepers. Where do you live, anyway?"

"Texas."

"Texas?" She chuckled then looked intently at Jack. "That's..." she pointed into the air and to her left. "What are you doing here!?"

Jack could tell she was confused. Heck, so was he.

"Beats me. That's what I'm trying to figure out. I went to some house a little ways off for some help and this dumb lady calls the cops on me, can you believe it?"

"You mean those cops are looking for *you*? Wow. Not cool. Wow, that's why there were all those police cars at my aunt's house when I passed it." Meagan's face looked like she had just made a revelation. She gave him a beaming smile.

"That was your aunt? The tall lady with the canary yellow blouse?"

"Yes. Her name is Mrs. Templeton. My other aunt lives in the third house from the end on the other side of the street. She's okay. Typical adult, though. You know. She tries to get into everyone else's business. What did you say to make her call the cops, anyway?" Meagan was smiling and her eyes gleamed with excitement as if she were on a bright new adventure.

Jack could see Meagan found this really interesting. Her blue eyes sparkled and, for some reason, he suddenly felt totally comfortable with her sitting there in front of him. It was strange, but it was like they had known each other forever and they came here all the time.

"I just told her I was lost, that's all. I thought I could just call my parents and that would be it."

"Well, what happened then?"

"I found out I was in Wright Wood, California and my phone number doesn't exist. What year is this?"

"You are wearing my shirt."

"I borrowed it. Sorry. Hope you don't mind. I only had my shorts on. I mean, I was in the water and all."

"What year is this? 2016, silly!" She retorted.

"Where I'm from it's 2014." Jack replied, then shivered over the notion that he shouldn't have told her that. Her face changed just like Mrs. Templeton's and he began to worry again.

"I told you that you wouldn't believe me," he said softly with dejection.

She stared at Jack's eyes a moment then nodded. Her expression tense.

"Wow. Okay."

He could tell she was evaluating him, debating in her head whether to believe it or not.

"Someone knock you on the head or something? Maybe you fell down somewhere? But listen, you can't stay here. You have to go, and you have to go now. Those policemen I saw are going to be here very fast.

"Look I know I sound crazy, but all I know is, I went to this pond in the woods by my house yesterday morning to think things out, you know? It's a place I go to that no one else knows about. The water is kind of hot in the pond, more like really warm. You know, one of those thermal springs or something. I saw this light in a tunnel in the water below a big tree. I was curious, so I swam through it. The only thing is, when I came out I was in your pond back yonder."

"There's no tunnel in that pond. And the water isn't warm, either."

"Yeah. Don't I know it. But you do know where I'm talking about, right?" Jack nodded and Meagan nodded back.

"Yeah. Rarely go there, though. There's a big ravine you gotta cross. Wow. That's really weird. So you think, I'm going to believe you came through a time warp or something? No one's going to believe that story. Hey, that pond is a good distance into the woods, but you can make it back, and I won't tell anyone I've seen you."

"Where am I going to go?"

"To that cave you talked about."

"Aw, c'mon, Meagan. Look at my feet." He rose and turned around raising his one foot for her to see the cuts. "I've already been chased by a mountain lion and nearly died." He lifted the shirt and struggled through the pain to show her his wound. Meagan grimaced.

He faced her again. "it's tough enough walking in the daylight where I can watch where I'm walking, but at night? And what happens if I run into another mountain lion?"

Meagan pondered for a long minute before she answered.

Jack sat and then stood up suddenly and Meagan recoiled with apprehension. He noticed just a flash of fear in her eyes.

"Look! This is the school I go to. Daley-Brammel. I'm on the football team." Jack pulled at his shorts where the school logo was.

"Never heard of it," she said looking closely at the name on his shorts and then gave his body the once over, noticing Jack was the same height as she.

"Yeah. That's what your aunt said. What's her name? She looked up the town I live in and it exists, at least."

"Mrs. Templeton," she repeated impatiently. Meagan pulled out her tablet from the backpack she had slid off her back and placed on the floor beside the chair when she sat down. What did you say the name of your school was?"

"Oh. Great. Uh - Daley-Brammel. Jack spelled it out for Meagan as she keyed it into the internet.

"Yep. Here it is. Daley-Brammel. Spring, Texas."

"Let me see the date on your tablet."

Meagan turned it around and Jack read the date. May 29, 2016. He shook his head and sighed heavily. "I was hoping it would say something else."

"Like 2014, right?"

Jack nodded.

"I really don't believe you, you know. I mean, this time thing and all, it's not working, but like I said, I will cover for you if you leave now." Meagan was not asking now, it was a demand. She quickly reached into her backpack. Standing up in one single motion she pulled out her pepper spray and pointed to Jack. "Get out now or I will empty the can on your face and get the police here before you can move again."

Jack jumped to his feet, pain coursing from his feet to his back. His arms outstretched towards her in a defensive plea.

"Please Meagan."

"Out!" she yelled, threateningly.

Jack swiftly moved around her and ran towards the door. Fear commanding the flight, despite the unknown and possible dangers.

Jack ran, wincing at the pain from his feet. He ran not knowing the direction in which he was going. Not paying attention, just trying to get away.

It wasn't long when Jack realized he wasn't the only one running. The loud thump from his heart came in so loud and heavy it was hard to hear anything else around him. Adrenaline rushed through his body propelling him to go faster, yet the prickling pain in his lungs burned as hot cinders rekindling with every breath, telling him he couldn't go much further. Branches gashed his limbs as he fought to make his way through, blood leaving more evidence of the trail for his pursuer. He had no plan to escape this, there hadn't been any time to think of one, all he could do for now was run, but that alone seemed futile in the end.

Jack was in trouble, and he had to do something to escape or conquer over his hunter. Running for his life it was hard to think of the path that landed him here; the speed of his footsteps over the hard terrain turned into a slow motion blur replaced by an easy stride over a paved street; one he knew well, one that had a sense of safety; his home street. The memory flashed on his mind for an instance, clearing as he tripped and landed on his back. The gash on his back splitting open, pain and blood oozed again.

Jack rubbed his eyes to clear his vision, blinking hard only to see before him, a swiftly and carefully approaching mountain lion. His right front leg had dried blood caked over his fur. This was the same lion that had chased him earlier. Alive, angry and back to finish the job. It was personal.

Jack reached for rocks and started throwing them at the lion. He had to get out. Fear gripped him. This was the end of the line for him. His lift flashed before his eyes. Jack was pinned though he worked to slide backwards as the cat approached him; walking slowly now, knowing it had won. Jack's arms moved to his side instinctively looking for a weapon of sorts. His fingers felt and found a stick. Jack gripped tight and readied for the worst.

The lion went to pounce and Jack rolled to his side clearing the cat's landing. He lanced and jabbed the stick at it, and as he turned to run Meagan flanked Jack spraying every bit of the pepper spray into the cat's face.

"Run Jack!" Meagan yelled over the screeching wail from the mountain lion's pain.

Both Meagan and Jack ran together as fast as they could. Jack was limping and struggling to keep up. Meagan came and scooped her body under and helped Jack to keep moving. "C'mon Jack, you gotta keep moving."

After what felt like an eternity both reached the cabin and slammed the door shut behind them. Dropping to their hands and knees, heaving air into their lungs. Jack heaved and threw up.

"I'm sorry Jack." said Meagan. "Are you ok?"

"You came for me!" Jack muttered in between heavy breaths. "Why?"

"I heard the lion hiss right after you ran out. I couldn't live with myself if something happened to you after I ran you out, right into it."

"Thank you." He said. Still fighting to control his breathing and keep from throwing up again.

"You're not going to turn into some really scary ugly alien or something are you?" Meagan feebly laughed.

Jack chuckled with her. Her smile was pretty. It seemed warm somehow and made him feel good. Relief poured over him at the sense of safety.

"Better be careful. I'm at least a thousand years old and can throw you around this room like a rag doll."

"Yeah. Dream on, Dracula. Maybe you're like that really old sci-fi flick where you're nothing but a blob—whose puke has to be cleaned—after we look at your wounds."

"I'm sure I won't enjoy either task." Jack said as his breath slowed and he became more aware of the pain from all the open gashes on his body.

"Maybe I can help you find your way back. You probably fell and bumped your head or something and just think it's 2014. We can go to the pond. Maybe we'll find something there that'll help you remember. By the way, what's your real name?"

"Jack West. I told you. Look it's right here on my shorts." Jack rose and pulled the waist band over and showed her the name hand written in black.

Meagan nodded. Standing up and motioning for Jack to the kitchen where she pulled a first aid kit from one of the shelves.

"You were really on the football team?"

"Yeah."

"What position?"

"Running back."

"Wow. Cool. I'm on the soccer team here."

"You play soccer? Really? Cool. I'm on the track team, too. Run the mile."

"I love football. My Dad, brother and I watch it together." Meagan said as she cleaned Jack's cuts and covered them with bandages and closed others with butterfly band-aids.

"I guess you're a 49er." Jack beamed through the pain, looking at the shirt he was wearing, now dirty and torn.

"Is there any other?" She smiled and Jack couldn't help but smile with her. The thought of her being pretty flashed through his mind again.

"Texans!"

"Gotta admit. Not bad. The team, I mean."

Jack nodded. "Ouch!" Jack winced as Meagan tugged to lift his shirt to work over his back.

"Don't tell me your Dad takes you to a sports bar or something to watch the games on Sunday, too?" Jack said. Megan raised an eyebrow in response.

"You know. A sports place. Chicken wings and burgers. The parents drink beer and they have all these televisions scattered around the room showing every one of the games. It gets really wild with everyone screaming and yelling and all."

"Yep, we have those in California My dad wants to go to Tommy's, but my Mom insists we stay at home. She doesn't like it when he drinks. It's pretty isolated out this way, anyway. There's only a local grocery store and a gas station with a convenience store herein town, about five miles away. But I like that. I don't like crowds; I'd rather be here in the woods where I feel more at home."

Jack nodded in agreement, thinking of his parents.

"We watch the games in the living room," Meagan continued. "My Mom doesn't care for football, so she just makes us some snacks and goes to her room and reads or watches TV. My dad, brother, and I do make a lot of noise though, especially when the 49ers score.

I love Sundays during football season." Her excitement faded as she shifted her thought.

"The pond is about an hour's walk. Hm-m," Meagan thought for a minute, then snapped out of it like she had the answer to a problem, but didn't say anything.

They continued talking about school and what they liked to do for a long time, as if they hadn't a care in the world. Their conversation changed to their parents and they exchanged their complaints about their home life.

"Well. I think I'd actually like doing chores around the house right now," Jack commented, shaking his head. It's better than being lost or chased twice in one day by a mountain lion. I never realized how important the family is until now, and how much your parents actually do for you."

"Well." Meagan shrugged. "Maybe you're right. Maybe it's not so bad."

Then Jack realized it was getting dark.

"Oh man. I need to get home. How am I going to make it back to the pond? We'll never make it there and back before it gets dark." Jack stood and looked outside. "Do you think it will come after me again?

Meagan rose and lit several candles and placed three of them on the table and one on the kitchen counter. "No. I'm pretty sure the burn from the spray has caused serious damage, and with no water to attempt to rinse off, I think it may have blinded him." She said. "Besides, it was injured on one leg pretty bad."

"Maybe I can leave early tomorrow to find the pond." Jack said.

"Okay, Jack. We'll stay here for the night, but you gotta sleep out here, and I'm going to lock my door."

"That kind of thought never crossed my mind. The floor is just fine with me. I'll leave in the morning."

"Boy. My parents think I'm at a girlfriend's house. I didn't tell my friend to say I'm sleeping over. I hope they don't call and check on me. They'll have a fit if I don't go home. Ground me. I hate that." Worry was written all over her face.

"By now mine are really worried. I should have been home yesterday."

"Yesterday?" Meagan questioned.

"Yeah. I slept by the pond last night, in just my swimming trunks. There was this little, uh, area like that was full of leaves."

"You slept in my bed!" She laughed, "I made that for whenever I explore up there. Wow. That was a long time ago. In summer it gets pretty hot. Smells good with all those leaves and everything, doesn't it?"

"Yes, it does. You're the first person I know that likes the woods the way I do. It's pretty cool." He said.

"Yeah. When my parents find out I'm not at my friend's house I gotta come up with a real doozy of an excuse."

"Hey, loan me your tablet? Maybe I can use the internet to chat with my friends? Get help."

"Sure. Good idea." Meagan said.

"I don't know why I didn't think of that before. That's really stupid. I'll just chat with my friends and tell them to get in touch of my parents and they can come for me. Problem solved."

"Yeah! Why didn't I think of that?" Meagan slid her tablet over to him and Jack began to pound on the keys, bright with anticipation.

Jack's forehead furrowed.

"What? Can't be." He typed some more.

It took less than three minutes to find out none of the emails of his friends existed. He fought the tears of desperation hard because he certainly didn't want to cry in front of Meagan. Was he going to be stuck here forever?

Why was all this happening? What kind of power does his pond have? Why was that cave there, shaped like that? Why is this cabin here? And why am I with this girl? Who sent her? Jack struggled for answers. Jack took a deep breath and let out a long sigh. _Is there a purpose to all this? Do I have anything to do with this?_

Meagan slowly took hold of the tablet and slid it back to her side of the table and turned it around to read the responses on the screen. She looked at Jack with sad eyes.

"Sorry, Jack," she said softly.

He simply nodded.

"But don't worry. We'll find an answer. Anyway, at least you don't have school to worry about, right?" Her voice returned to its bubbly self.

Jack looked into Meagan's smiling face. Even in the candlelight he could see her complexion was smooth, he hadn't taken notice of that before. She made him feel better; and somehow she made him feel like everything would turn out all right. He felt he had found a friend, a friend that maybe would be there for him, like he was for Red.

Jack nodded. "School's out where I'm from. Friday was the last day."

"Yeah. That's right. Here, too. Oh, I brought some more food. Hungry? I am. There's plenty. I always bring extra to leave on the shelf."

"I noticed."

"Yes. And you helped yourself to it, too! When this is over you owe me. I expect you will send me what you ate," Meagan chuckled waving her index finger at him with a smile.

They both laughed. Meagan picked up her backpack, set it on her chair, and began pulling out items and putting them away. Jack sat watching her.

"Why don't you tell me your whole story from the beginning? Maybe I can figure something out. There's always a solution." Said Meagan.

She sounded so confident. He really liked that about her.

They talked till well past midnight. Meagan told Jack her parents had never hit her; however, they grounded her a lot. Jack told Meagan about the times he and his Mom and Dad went camping and fishing, but now their lives were occupied with their friends. During their long conversation, Meagan dubbed Jack's pond the Magic Pond and Meagan's pond the Wright Pond. They played around with Jack's predicament, making a story of it, so Meagan said they had to name their ponds to know which was which. Jack's was imaginary so it was the Magic Pond and Meagan's was real so it was the right pond, of course she explained she had to spell it in a way to be different, so a "W" would be appropriate.

Jack gave Meagan all the details of his first encounter with the mountain lion to which she paid the closest attention, interrupting his explanation with a lot of questions.

Meagan told Jack about her friends, even though she didn't have many because she was called a tomboy. She talked about the soccer team, how she was a very good player, which Jack believed. Meagan even shared with Jack her fascination for insects and how she made herself a little lab in her bedroom and Jack soaked up her every word as if it were gospel, especially fascinated that she had all those insects in her bedroom. There was something about her that just made him feel she was as honest as the day was long. She was real.

"So how did you find this cabin, anyway?" Jack queried.

"Actually, it was by accident. I had gotten to the ravine one day in summer, I think it was about four years ago. I remember going over that fallen tree across the ravine. It was early. I then came across that pond, Wright Pond, she smiled, and I was tired so I made a little shelter and gathered a bunch of leaves to rest on. I actually fell asleep for just a little while. I didn't use your idea of stick men, good idea, by the way, I had a compass. As I came back, even with a compass you can't come back exactly like you went, I came across this cabin. I found a key on top of the doorframe. I've been coming here ever since."

"No one's ever come here? You know, the real owners?"

"Nope. And I have no idea who it belongs to, and don't want to know. Hope they never come." She said idly.

As the night wore on, Meagan opened up further and shared with Jack about some of the scrapes she had gotten into with the police. She had been caught stealing some candy from the convenience store and the employee actually detained her and called the police. She told him about her grades, which were good, and her teachers; who like Jack's, were sometimes good and sometimes bad.

Then it was Jack's turn to open up. He told Meagan, again, about how his parents used to be great; how they all used to go camping together, but that now his mom and dad just drank with their friends on weekends and sometimes even during the week. Jack continued on how the house and their clothes always reeked from the cigarettes, something that really bothered him.

"Oh my Goodness, look at the time!" Meagan said with a jolt of realization. "It's so late! Oh, man. Look at the candles! They're almost gone," Meagan she ended with delight and rose to bring some new ones.

"Don't you just hate parents?" Meagan said in a soft sad tone, her eyes drifting to the wooden tabletop.

"C'mon Meagan. You don't really mean that."

Jack looked down on the table and said as if reading a book, "Honor thy father and thy mother."

Meagan looked at him, her head tilted just a little sideways, as Jack noticed she did anytime she had a question.

"It's what my minister would say. We used to go to church every Sunday, but my parents sleep in now."

Meagan looked at Jack with questioning eyes. Jack didn't strike her as one of those fanatical religious people. She knew some grownups that were always quoting the Bible, yet their lives were really messed up. They used drugs; had children without being married; been in jail; were alcoholics; or who knows what else. But she had never met a person her age that was

seemingly religious. Kids went to church with their
parents because they had to, just as she did, but they
hardly ever mentioned God otherwise, much less quote
from scripture.

"That's what I was taught in church, also." she explained with a thin smile. "Yeah, well that's when
they are good parents, right?"

"I've been thinking about that—Why? Why do
parents always have to be good? Are we always good?
I think the words have nothing to do with whether parents are good or bad, dumb or smart, or anything else."
Jack said.

Meagan looked at Jack. She didn't quite understand what he was trying to say.

"Look. When you grow up and have kids, you're
gonna want them to respect you, aren't you?"

"Well, yeah. But I'm gonna treat them right."

"Good for you. And I think you will, too. But not
all parents are the same. Some need help." He added.

"How am I gonna help my parents? I have no control over what they do." A hint of disdain permeated
Meagan's tone.

"If we help them, we will be showing them we respect them. Remember, I said that things used to be
different, that they were once great parents?"

"Yeah. But that was then, and this is now." She in-
terjected.

"If we can somehow help our parents, somehow
show them what they're doing wrong. Maybe I can get

mine to be like they were before and maybe you can get yours to understand you better."

"I don't know, Jack. Maybe we do think about only ourselves."

"Right. As time goes on, and if everything goes right, our parents become more successful. Which is good, right? But then the people they work for give them more responsibility, which they accept to make more money so we can live better, or at least the same. My Dad keeps telling me things get more expensive every year to do the same things. I think they get caught up in work, you know, trying to keep making more money? They kind of forget us 'cause they gotta work so much."

Meagan just looked at Jack, the candlelight dancing on her cheeks.

"Okay, okay. So how am I going to help them?"

"I don't know, yet." He said.

"See!?" Desire met with frustration was evident on Meagan's face.

"To start with, I guess we could talk to them, tell 'em how we feel, you know?"

"Well yeah. My Dad would listen. But my Mom? She's like a dictator. Get my head knocked off is what I'd be getting. I'm not suicidal. But hey, I'd be the first headless student in school. That would make me popular, right? You know, maybe I could talk out of my navel...'hi there, guys. What's goin' on up there?' 'Course then everyone would be lookin' down at me all the time. Geez. When I go to the bathroom, my mouth would be at a very precarious level. Oh no. Forget it. I'm not talkin' to my Mom. Nope."

Jack laughed at Meagan's comments.

"Well, there you go. You'd be famous. I'm sure your Mom's not that bad, either. So start with your Dad and ask him how to talk with your Mother." He suggested precociously.

They both laughed. Meagan was so easy to talk to.

"Which of your parents is easier to talk to, Jack. Your Mom or Dad?"

"That's easy. Mom."

"For me it's my Dad, for sure."

"So, like I said, start with him."

"They won't listen, you know."

She looked at Jack with 'disappointed' written all over her face.

"So you're gonna give up? Without even trying? I guess I was wrong about you. I thought you were strong, not just like in the muscles, in the brain, in the heart. The girl who will rescue a friend and face a mountain lion! And boy, you were tough on me when you came in here; how can you give up so easily? I know what I'm going to do; I'm going to tell my parents exactly how I feel and tell them we should go camping or do something together, like we used to."

He felt a sudden anxiety in his chest. He wanted, no, he needed Meagan's approval, because he still wasn't really sure about himself.

"Hey! I am strong!" She stood and flexed her arms taking on a position like Mr. Universe.

"Is that all there is?" Jack said and they laughed loudly and he joined her with a pose of his own.

"Okay. Maybe you're right. But what if it doesn't work?"

"You keep trying until it does, I guess. And I'm sure it won't work right away. They'll probably shoot you down, maybe three, four times. But, eventually, you'll get through. Ask your minister for advice." Jack said.

"Uh, I'm not exactly that close to him."

"You don't have to be, Meagan. He'll help you even if you're a complete stranger. That's what they do. Help people."

"Really think so?" Unbelief covered her face.

"Know so. Besides, that's their job. They take an oath, just like medical doctors. They get paid to do that."

"Well. Maybe you're right. Now that we figured everything out, all we have to do is get you home."

"Yeah. There's still that detail. One step at a time, I guess." Jack thought of his Dad. He missed his advice. He missed being with him.

Jack and Meagan finally decided to go to bed, not because they were really that tired, but because it was so late. Meagan handed Jack a couple of blankets and a pillow, then closed the bedroom door. Jack heard her lock it.

"Ha, ha," Jack laughed out loud.

"What's so funny?" Meagan yelled through the door.

"Oh, no. Never mind."

"Oh no you don't. Tell me."

"Well. I have this friend. Red. He's always talking about girls. He's in Cancun right now. He told me he'd kiss one of the chicks for me— among other things."

"I hate guys like that. And he's your friend?"

"I'm afraid he is. Best friend, actually."

"So what's so funny?"

"If he knew I was sleeping with a girl— ha, ha."

Meagan bolted upright and peeled the door open, anger flashing through her face.

"You're not! And promise me you're not going to tell anyone!"

"Of course not. I promise. Besides, who would believe me?"

Meagan closed the door and slowly sank into her pillow and smiled. Jack was right. Who would believe him?

They continued to talk through the door a few more minutes. It felt like he was camping out with a friend. Jack had to admit with profound embarrassment, he knew he would fall asleep before Meagan did.

Tomorrow Jack would try to find the tunnel again, but this time around he had help.

"Jack?" Came the voice behind the door.

"Yes." He replied.

"Don't forget to clean-up the mess by the front door."

"Oh...Yeah...that mess." Jack sighed and wished he didn't have to face the throw-up. The likelihood that he'd do it again due to the sheer grossness of having to clean it made him cringe. He pressed his eyes shut tight and took a deep breath. He would now have to face the mess, and in dread headed for the supplies he would need to clean it, hoping he'd survive this part of the day.

CHAPTER 8

The Tunnel

My world threatens to come to an end
When finally I find the tunnel's light
unwittingly I involve a friend
That unselfishly helps me with my plight

The morning light crept through the window and filtered gently through a thin piece of an old pink sheet that Meagan had rescued from the garbage at home after her Mother had thrown it out, hung with three nails from above the window. Jack stirred and turned over.

"What the...?" He came to his feet quickly. Jack's mind filled with yesterday's memories like the start of the faucet filling the bathtub. Everything was familiar yet he had to wait for it to fill its memory bank up to put things back into perspective.

Had he dreamed this wild adventure? It was as if he was almost floating in some sort of limbo and was fighting to find reality, some kind of solid surface to stand on.

He looked at the closed bedroom door.

Jack smiled, looked at the light coming through the pink material that hung lazily over the window, then knocked on the door. This was real, at least in some fashion.

"I'm up." said Meagan.

Jack shook his head, raised his arms, stretched this way and that and then shuffled his way into the kitchen to look for something to eat.

He dug through the shelves and saw Meagan had brought some fresh sliced ham.

"Great," he whispered.

He remembered seeing a loaf of bread somewhere, yes, there it was, on the same shelf to the left. He spotted and grabbed the small jar of mayonnaise, the ham, and the bread and set them on the table and began to prepare himself a sandwich.

"Make it two if you're going to eat my food," Meagan said as she entered the kitchen area.

"Oh!" Jack said in a startled voice dropping the knife on the table while bringing his left hand up to his chest. He turned to see Meagan standing in the ray of light from the uncovered window towards the back of the house. The light seemed to hang around her body and gave the impression she was glowing.

"What?" Meagan looked at herself to see if there was something in disarray, then ran her hands through her golden locks and shook her head.

"Am I that bad? I just got out of bed, you know." She continued to try to fix her hair.

She moved out of the light and sat at the table.

"There's some sports drinks if you want," she said matter-of-factly.

Jack seemed relieved when she stepped out of the window's direct light, but nonetheless it took another minute to collect himself.

"Oh. Ah, yeah, sure." He pulled two more slices of bread out of the bag and spread mayonnaise on both slices.

"So what are you gonna do, Jack?"

Meagan's question was absolutely logical, but it caught him somewhat by surprise. He actually hadn't thought about his plan of action yet. It was as if he was on a camping trip with Meagan. Jack felt completely comfortable with her. Actually, he felt more comfortable with her than any of his friends, even Red.

He looked at Meagan and shrugged.

"Don't know." He finished making the sandwiches and gave Meagan one, then went to the shelf, picked up the sports drinks, and took a seat opposite his host. A small part of him hinted at wanting this fantasy to continue forever.

"I think—no, I know, the secret is at the pond. We need to go to the pond." Jack added.

"Okay, but you know the police will probably be looking for you today."

"The police? Why? I didn't hurt anyone, steal anything, I didn't do anything wrong." He took a big bite of his sandwich and chewed while keeping his eyes on Meagan.

"Well, from what you told me, they probably think you're lost *and* a little screwy upstairs, know what I mean?"

Jack looked at her quizzically.

"You told them you were from another place, re-member? That you came from Texas, somewhere, and this is California. You're a minor. They're not going to simply say you are some kind of weirdo adult and forget it."

"You really think so?"

"C'mon, Jack. It's logical. Maybe I should make you some coffee, well, if we had any." Meagan smiled and took a bite of her sandwich. "Not bad," Meagan continued. "They'll probably organize a small search party and start combing the woods."

"Do they know about this place?"

"If they don't, sooner or later they'll stumble on it." She pondered and shook her head.

"What?" He asked.

"If they find this place then I won't have a place to go to."

Jack looked at her. Meagan's cheeks were lightly splattered with freckles just under the eyes; so light, he had not even noticed them last night. He felt guilty about the possibility of Meagan losing her secret place.

"Well. We can hide everything and make it look abandoned, you know? I mean, they'll just forget about it, won't they? After a couple of weeks, I mean."

"Maybe. We can try. But first I think we better concentrate on finding out how you are going to get back home. Now, let's find this tunnel of yours, okay?"

"Yeah. You're right." Jack replied.

Meagan rose and put what was left of their drinks in her backpack. Then they tidied up the cabin, folded the blanket and stored them along with the pillows back in the chest, and put all the dishes in their respective places, just in case.

"Thanks," Jack said as they left the house. Meagan looked at him.

"For the food, and the bed, and for being a friend."

She nodded, turned away from him and smiled.

"You know, you are right. I could make my situation at home much better. The pond is this way," Meagan stated pointing to the right. "You did come from this way, right?"

"Yeah. What do you mean, you can make your situation better? What are you talking about?"

Meagan stopped in her tracks and stared at Jack.

"You're the one who told me! Last night, remember? We're not kids any more, Jack, are we? Have

you ever really tried to help your parents? I haven't."
Meagan felt she had matured so much since yesterday.

They continued to walk in silence for a while.

"How are you going to help them? I mean, well, you know."

"I'll just have to sit them down and talk with them, just like you said. I guess it can't really be that bad, right? I really want my Mom to love me, for who I am, not who she wants me to be. I want her to see me and like me, instead of the pictures she has drawn in her mind of who I ought to be. Maybe we could meet in the middle; perhaps if she steps into my world, I can step into hers and find a common ground to be more than just mother and daughter at odds. We could have a relationship. I think we can compromise without changing who we are inside. Besides, I just gotta do my chores. Maybe she could list them so I can get them done faster. Kind of like doing homework. Get it out of the way so you can play."

Jack laughed.

"What's so funny about that?"

Jack shook his head, "Nothing. You sound, and I feel, older than I did before I met you. Does that make any sense?"

Meagan nodded.

"Yeah. Actually it does. It's like a year passed since yesterday."

"Exactly! Look! There's one of my stick men," Jack pointed proudly.

"Hey, that's cool, Jack." She bent down to pick it up. "I'll have to remember this." She nodded her approval, and then threw it away.

"No, don't! How will we find our way back?"

She looked at him with disbelief.

"Jack! If we can follow these stickmen, so can the police. Besides. I know my way around. Remember? I really don't need your stick men to find the pond. We're just tracing your steps."

"Oh. Yeah. I guess you're right." Jack felt more than a little dumb.

"I know these woods. Don't worry."

"I hope so," Jack said softly and Meagan chuckled softly to herself.

"You know there are places you can go for therapy to get your mind back too, you know, normal and all. All you gotta do is convince yourself to try it."

"You still don't believe me, do you? There's another one!"

She bent down, picked it up and threw it into the woods.

"You know, on my way back I should make some of these and mark a trail *away* from the house. Maybe I can make the police avoid the cabin."

"Wow. Good idea, Meagan." Jack wanted to say she was pretty smart, but decided to bite his tongue.

"When we get to the pond I'll prove it to you, that I'm not imagining things, I hope anyway." What was he going to do if the tunnel still wasn't there.

No! It'll be there. The answer is there. It has to be! He glanced at Meagan in case he had spoken out loud.

"Really? Well. Don't worry, Jack. We'll find a solution anyway, okay?"

Jack nodded and they pushed on. The morning sun filtered through the multitude of branches and its warmth felt good. There was no breeze and the air was filled with music provided by the birds that fluttered here and there playing in the treetops. They didn't really walk, they strolled, like a couple going through a park, without the romance, of course. The atmosphere of the woods and his newfound friend seemed to shrink Jack's problem.

Meagan would occasionally stop and show Jack some insect and give a small history of it. He enjoyed it. He had to admit, she really knew her bugs.

"You got the guts to face your parents when you get home?"

"Who—me?"

"Yeah. It's not goin' to be easy. Sounds difficult, anyway. You can make excuses, but they won't believe anything you say, anyway, so you might as well tell them the truth. You said you were a football player. Be tough with them. You love them, don't you?" Meagan asked.

Jack stopped and stared at her. He was trying to figure out where that had just come from. Just when you think you know a girl, she says something from out of left field.

"There's another stick man. Should only be three or four more. Pretty smart making these, right?"

"Yes. It was. So do you?" Meagan pressed.

"Do I what?"

"You're avoiding the question. You love your parents, don't you?"

"Well, sure. They're my parents."

"So I figure they probably will listen to how you feel."

"You make it sound so easy."

"Well, I imagine we'll both get nervous talking to them and all that. And at first, they will probably get angry and tell us lots of junk like, 'don't tell me how to be a better parent,' and stuff like that."

"That's for sure!" Boy she was really thinking hard about their talk last night.

"When you want something, do you keep after them until they give up and give it to you?"

"Ha, ha. Yeah. I remember when I wanted my iPhone. Took me weeks to convince them." Jack reached down and pulled the stick man from out of the ground and tossed it deep into the woods.

"There's the ravine," Meagan announced. She came to the edge and looked down. "So this is where you first encountered the mountain lion?"

"See the big tree anywhere?" Jack looked down the current. "There! Boy! We came right to it, almost."

They hurried downstream and peered into the water below.

"Where? I don't, oh, yes. I see it. Wow. You were right, Jack?"

Meagan looked straight into Jack's eyes. "I didn't believe anything you said, despite saving your rear from the mountain lion. I just really thought it was coincidence, or that you had seen it around." She looked below. "I'm beginning to change my mind, but I still don't believe your Magic Pond, okay?"

"Okay, okay. You'll see." Jack was hoping very hard she would see he was not lying.

"Let's find a place to cross. Now that you destroyed the bridge," Meagan accused.

"Would you rather I was eaten by that lion?"

"There!" Meagan pointed a little further downstream, and began to jog, Jack right on her heels not knowing what she was referring to.

Meagan stopped by a large tree and looked up.

"See? We can climb across that large limb to the other side."

"Isn't it a little high?"

"When we get to the other side, the branch will bend. We'll be able to jump off. I'll go first."

Meagan shimmied up the tree and made her way across the large limb with ease. She inched her way once over land until the branch began to bend towards the ground. Little by little she continued, then she jumped and Jack took a sharp breath. She landed safely on the other side.

"Okay, Jack. Your turn."

Jack copied her moves and found it was easier than he thought, landing on his feet on the other side, but the flip-flops slid and he went down to the ground with a thud. Wincing from all the wounds from the previous day he took a breath and picked himself up quickly.

"It's over this way," Meagan said and they continued.

"You keep practicing football until you've got it right, correct?" Meagan began.

"Yep. That's how you get to be the best."

"That's what we will do to help them."

Jack stopped and looked at Meagan.

"How could she be so smart for just a girl? She had turned the tables and was now giving him advice." He remembered his dad mentioning something about women being good at turning a man's words around. This was probably what he meant.

Meagan sensed his stopping and turned around.

"Are you coming? Or do you see the pond?" She smiled knowingly, and then quickly cast her eyes around the woods in search for water.

"No. I'm coming. Can't be far now."

"So do your parents really drink a lot now?"

"No. Well, I don't think so. I mean, they never get really drunk and all that. My Mom gets tipsy sometimes. I hate when she does that. She gets all mushy and stuff, you know?"

"Really? I wish my Mom would get mushy. I think my teacher is nicer to me."

"Isn't that the pond over there?" Meagan winked at Jack and quickened her pace with Jack after her.

"There it is, Jack. Actually, I had kind of forgotten this was here until you mentioned it yesterday. I haven't been here since last summer. It's so far away."

Meagan felt the water.

"Wow. That is cool, Jack, just like you said. I wonder where the water comes from. Didn't you say it was hot in your pond?

"Not on your side. Only the other side."

"The Magic Pond side. Right. The Wright Pond is cold. The tunnel, Jack. You see it?"

Jack took a deep breath and sighed heavily, shaking his head. He had already been looking for it.

Meagan read the disappointment in his face.

"Whereabouts was it. Remember?"

"Over there by that big tree on the right. See the big roots?"

They slowly made their way to the tree. Jack slipped off Meagan's shower shoes and sat down on the big root that erupted from the ground and stepped into the water. He put his head in his hands supported by his knees, staring into the water, hoping a light would appear.

"What are you gonna do now?" Meagan asked.

"Don't know." He fought the tears of frustration back.

"Oh, no!" Meagan said abruptly.

"What?" Jack said looking up, bewildered.

"Hear that?"

"Yeah. People talking."

"The police!" Meagan declared.

"We had better hide," Jack said getting up, then he froze staring into the water.

"Jack! C'mon!" Meagan yelled in a whisper.

"Look, Meagan!" Jack pointed at the water below the large tree. He slid into the water and positioned himself between the two large roots of the tree, then looked up at Meagan.

Her eyes widened. "I'm sorry, I didn't believe you," she whispered.

"I gotta go," he said softly, but his heart, along with every other fiber of his body pulled at him to stay.

"Go. Good luck, Jack." Meagan wanted to give Jack a hug, but just couldn't, because her feet were frozen to the spot where she stood.

"I'll be back. I promise."

"I hope so. Better go! They're getting closer!"

"Yeah, thanks, you know."

"Yes, I know. You're welcome. Now go!"

Jack slid deeper into the cold water. His eyes got big and his lips puckered.

Ooh, that's really cold! He thought to himself.

Meagan smiled. "Cold?" she said knowing he couldn't answer.

Jack just nodded his head, and looked below. The light was there. He looked up at Meagan. She smiled and nodded, and Jack could swear he saw her eyes were watery. His chest hurt. He really didn't want to go but the light tugged at him strongly, like a powerful magnet that was just too strong to resist pulling him in.

I'll be back. Jack took in all the air his lungs could hold and ducked into the tunnel, then disappeared into the light.

Meagan heard the voices were very close. It was too late to run and hide. They burst through the trees on the opposite side of the pond, stopped and stared at her sitting on the same root Jack had sat on a few minutes earlier, her feet dangling in the water

"Meagan? What are you doing here?"

It was her uncle, one of the local police officers. There were five other townspeople with him.

"Hi Uncle Dale. What are you doing here? I come here to be alone and think sometimes. Nice, isn't it?"

"A long ways from home just to think, isn't it? That's spring water. Too cold to swim in, wouldn't you say?"

Meagan looked into the water, quickly remembering the light. It was gone. She smiled.

"Yes, Uncle Dale. Too cold to swim," she said calmly.

"Throwing rocks into the pond, eh?"

She looked at him quizzically.

"Ripples in the water. You're not wet. Detective work," he bragged in front of the others, turning his head in their direction and winking.

They smiled and Meagan nodded in agreement with his explanation.

"So what are you all doing in the woods, Uncle Dale?"

"You haven't heard? Some kid stopped by your aunt's place with some crazy story about being from Texas and lost. Then he ran off into the woods. We're just trying to find him, help him get back home. You see anyone out here?"

Meagan shook her head slowly. *And he was from 2014, Uncle Dale,* she thought to herself and smiled.

"Nope."

"We saw a cabin back a ways. Seems he may have been holed up in there for a bit," one of the townsfolk offered.

"We don't really know. The door was locked," her Uncle Dale added.

Meagan shrugged her shoulders in ignorance, but her gut tied up into a knot.

"Aren't you afraid to come into the woods alone?" another one of the searching party asked?

"Naw. Do it all the time. It's peaceful."

"Know what you mean, Sweetheart," her uncle said.

"She's like me, nature lover," her uncle boasted to the others.

"Well. We gotta keep looking, Meagan. You should go home. It's a good hike back, and it's not safe, right now."

"Oh, ok, Uncle Dale. I'll make my way back then," she lied, amused.

"Let's go folks." Dale said leading them past Meagan.

"Maybe he got his senses back and went home," one of the townsfolk said as they disappeared into the woods.

Meagan let out a big sigh. She looked down into the water and smiled.

"Good luck, Jack. Goodbye."

Something told her she would never see him again and she felt melancholy.

Uncle Dale hadn't mentioned her Mother was looking for her, so she guessed Am had covered for her and told her Mother she was staying overnight somehow. She'd have to call Am to see what story she was going to tell her parents. Maybe the police officers and other towns people would forget about the cabin. Probably not. The owner would get news someone was using it and come out and lock it up tight.

No mention was made by anyone about the mountain near the cabin, either. If her Mother ever heard about that, the woods would be off limits *forever*. She wondered how they got across the ravine for a moment, then shrugged. She might as well start back.

I hope there aren't any more wild animals of any kind out here. Better get across that ravine that's only a short ways from here.

"Maybe I could build myself a tree house?" Meagan said softly to herself as she put her shoes back on and began to make her way back home. Somewhere nobody would find it, not even a search party. *Hmmm that has some cons to it.* She thought.

As she rose to her feet she spotted the flip-flops Jack had left on the bank. She bent down, grabbed a rock and placed it on top of the shower shoes. Smiling to herself, she nodded. They would be there for him if he ever came back. She never liked them anyway.

CHAPTER 9

Forgotten Details

The minds of children sometimes go astray
This doesn't make them bad in any way
If given the right direction to bear
They may enlighten you and their life you can share

Meagan stopped at the cabin and hid all the food under the bed, then swept the cabin clean and picked up the garbage bag they had left by the door.

She slipped on her backpack and, with the trash bag in her left hand, turned at the door and gave the cabin one last look. Meagan sighed heavily, closed the door behind her and locked it. She took a few steps and turned back to look at the cabin.

"I guess I gotta give you a break for a while. But I'll be back. You can bet on it. As soon as my Mom lifts the grounding." She turned and began walking.

She sighed heavily. Her stomach was in knots just at the thought of facing her parents.

Halfway home she hid the garbage bag in the woods. By the time Meagan came to the clearing where the street starts, her back was wet with perspiration, her face red from the exercise. She casually walked to her house, opened the garage door, dropped off her backpack by the door to the kitchen, pushed the button to close the garage and stepped inside the house.

There she was met by her whole family, all dressed up. Meagan closed her eyes. They hadn't gone to church. Oh, was she in trouble.

"Meagan!" her Mother roared. "Where in the hell were you!"

Her Mother had taken the Superwoman stance again and her eyes threw the sharpest knives she had ever felt. Tyler smiled in the knowledge that his sister was really in for it. Her Dad just looked on calmly, relief in his face.

"I'm sorry, Mom. I forgot about church," Meagan lied.

"And worse, you lied to me! You used your friends to lie to me!"

"Yes, yes. I know. And you're right. I know you are going to ground me and it's all right. I deserve it. I'm really, really sorry I worried you. I had gone to the woods; up by the pond." She wasn't telling a lie now was she? "It was so nice up there. I was collecting some insects and I fell asleep. There's a little niche with a lot of leaves. It was so comfortable. Uncle Dale woke me up. Then I came home."

"Uncle Dale? Why was he up there?"

"He told me he was looking for some lost kid that Aunt Templeton had reported to him. He was with a handful of local town folk who volunteered, I guess."

"She's right about that, Dear. He called and asked if I wanted to join the search, but I said I couldn't," her Dad supported.

"See? See how dangerous it is in those woods? You don't know what or who's in there. Lord only knows what can happen to you. I forbid you to go there again! Consider yourself grounded for a month!"

Her Mother waited for the usual backtalk from her daughter, prepared to put her in her place.

"Yes, ma'am. I'm sorry I made everyone miss church," Meagan said softly and apologetically. She saw Tyler give her a thumbs up and wanted to ask him what he meant.

Her Mother stood speechless. She dropped her hands to her side and then braced herself on the back of a chair.

Her Dad came over to her.

"Your Mother was very worried. We all were. But you're here now. That's what's most important. Just try to be more considerate in the future." He hugged her.

"Uh. I think you better take a shower, young lady," he said stepping back.

"Oh. Yeah. I stink."

"You sure do," Tyler chimed in.

"That's enough out of you, young man," his Mother scolded. "Or maybe you'd like to join your sister in her punishment?"

He held his hands up in surrender, shook his head, and then motioned zipping his lip.

"May I go take a shower now, Mom?"

She nodded her permission and watched Meagan leave the living room.

"Something must have happened out there in those woods," she said softly to her husband.

"Don't go reading things that aren't there, Dear. She looks fine. You know how she is. She loves those woods. She loves the outdoors. She'll grow out of it, Dear."

"Didn't you see how she answered me?"

Theodore looked confused.

"I thought she was very respectful with you."

"Exactly! That's not normal. She didn't argue with me. She always has some smart comment to make. Something has happened, that's not our daughter!"

Theodore rolled his eyes. "Exaggerating," he said softly.

"I heard that! You always take her side. That's why she is always so rebellious! You need to put your foot down with her and stop being so nice. You're ruining her!"

Susan stomped around the kitchen and started banging pots and pans around in her preparation of lunch.

"Aren't we going out to lunch? We always go out to lunch," Tyler said.

"Not anymore!"

"C'mon, Dear. You don't want to cook. It's Sunday, your day off. We're all dressed up, Meagan will be ready shortly. Relax. Everything's okay now. There's no reason for you to have to make lunch. And we can go to the evening service. You won't miss a thing."

Her husband smiled, then walked over to her and put his arms around her waist from behind. "All's well that ends well," he whispered in her ear. "And you're still the most beautiful woman in the world."

She smiled and then abruptly pulled herself away from his embrace.

"I'd make Meagan stay home, but there's no one here to take care of her. She'd probably run off again." Susan began to put things away.

"She doesn't need a…" Tyler began, but his Father put his finger to his lips to stop what he knew he was going to say.

"Instead of the pancake house, how about we go to the spaghetti house today, Dear?" Theodore asked.

"Yeah!" Tyler piped.

"The spaghetti house?" Mother shrugged her shoulders and nodded. "Okay. If you want. You two didn't do anything wrong. No sense in you all having a punishment for something Meagan did. However, I'm going to give her so many chores she won't have time to think of those blasted bugs! And I'm calling Dale to verify her story, too."

"Of course, Dear."

Meagan had finished her shower and slipped on a pair jeans and a bright green slip over blouse. She stood looking at herself in her bedroom mirror, brushing her hair, then stopped and hung her arms at her side.

"Please make it through the tunnel, Jack," she whispered staring into the mirror. *He won't be back, will he? Have you ever seen a movie where someone goes through a portal and comes out at the same place twice? You're all right, Jack. Braver than others your age, and you seem smarter somehow, too.* She nodded to herself in the mirror. *He was a nice guy, even liked the woods.*

"Meagan!" Came the cry from afar.

"Coming, Mom!"

CHAPTER 10

The Adventure Ends

If at first you don't succeed, try, try again
A saying he'd heard now and then
But your world will definitely get better it's true
If you just muster your courage and do, do, do

Jack grabbed at the slippery sides of the tunnel, clasping roots whenever he could find one to pull him through the tunnel. He learned he could get through faster by pulling hard and slow instead of trying to pull himself through fast. It seemed surprisingly easy this time and he could feel the warmer water just before he cleared the other side and surfaced with air to spare in his lungs. He looked about anxiously. The water felt as warm as bath water. There, in front of the log, just where he left them two days ago, were his backpack and clothes draped over the large tree trunk.

Jack blinked his eyes several times and looked all around him, hanging onto the giant root of the tree, then back at the log. Yes. Everything was still there, exactly as he had left it. He was home.

"Yes!" He yelled.

He looked up through teary eyes into the sky and, through the multitude of colored leaves and the green thistles of the pines, the sun still giving light onto his secret pond, but it seemed much later than it was on the other side. The sun seemed close to setting.

Jack swam over towards his clothes and felt bottom. He stood and walked out of the pond, feeling the slippery mud ooze through his toes, and sat himself wearily on the fallen tree trunk beside his clothes. It was at this moment that Jack's emotions caught up to him. He began to cry, not just a couple of small tears to tickle his cheeks as they made their way down to the corner of his mouth, but big tears that flowed from his eyes and shook his body. He couldn't control his body as he sobbed out loud, until he was able to re-gain his composure, little by little; his body resting and his breathing returning to normal again. He took a couple of deep breaths and wiped the tears and his nose. Jack looked around one more time making sure that there was no one to be seen. Letting out a big sigh he smiled remembering this was why he came here in the first place. He could yell, say whatever he wanted, and yes, cry, and no one would ever know.

Jack reached into his backpack and pulled out his phone. He pushed the button on the side of the dark blue phone and the screen lit up. 5:37pm appeared in large white numbers. Saturday, June 3, 2014, appeared below the time in smaller white letters and numbers.

"What?" He looked around anxiously.

"Did I fall asleep? Dream all this?"

Jack felt his body, it was wet. He looked at his shirt, it was Meagan's shirt with 2016 on it. He sighed with mixture of relief and confusion. At least he wasn't crazy. He called home. There was no answer.

Jack walked over and looked into the pond. The light of the tunnel was gone.

Was that it? Was this 'Magic Pond' a one-time thing? Or did he just imagine and daydream all this. But how did he get this shirt then? No, no. He didn't dream this. He wore the proof. He looked around bewildered and slowly walked back to the log.

Jack pulled the wet shirt off and was going to put it in his backpack, but then stopped short. *How was he going to explain the shirt to his parents?* He looked around again then shook his head and put the shirt on the log. He stripped off his shorts and changed into dry clothes. Jack then grabbed the wet clothes and began walking the circumference of the pond, searching.

Not more than ten feet from the pond, Jack came upon a fallen tree that leaned against another. He formed a small shelter with some branches and leaves. He had to stoop down a little to get in, but entered and arranged a couple of branches to hang his clothes on to dry. Jack then stepped out of his little hideaway, but after taking only a few steps, he turned around, then went back and broke off some branches with leaves to create more cover. Once again, Jack stepped back a few steps and nodded. Unless someone actually crawled in there, they would not see the hanging clothes in there.

Jack decided he'd come back for them tomorrow. They would be dry by then. In the meantime, he would search for a really good hiding place for the shirt at home. Just for a second, a thought flashed through Jack's mind of the shirt being valuable, but Jack let it slip right back out. He would never give up that shirt, not in a million years.

Hey. Maybe I could bet on the 49ers winning the Super Bowl in 2016, and win myself some money," he thought. Then Jack shook his head and chuckled to himself. He'd probably lose somehow.

He dug a small bag of pretzels out of his pack and slung the backpack onto his back. Jack slowly started walking home, absent-mindedly munching on his snack. *Did his Magic Pond have a time tunnel that could send him to the future? The past? Should he try again? What if he got caught in the future or past and couldn't get back?* His mind was so preoccupied that he veered off course more than once on the way back to the edge of the woods. There was some kind of significance to his Magic Pond, he could feel it, but he just couldn't figure it out, at least not yet.

When he got home he made himself a sandwich with four slices of ham, a slice of cheese, a sliced tomato, and a couple of leaves of lettuce. Jack generously spread some mayonnaise on both slices of whole wheat bread.

He had just sat himself at the kitchen table and was about to make a private toast to Meagan when his Mother came through the door.

"Hi Sweetheart. Do your homework?"

His stomach did a flip as she passed him. She reeked of cigarettes. He set his sandwich down on the plate without taking the first bite. Jack was so glad to see her yet the smell had repulsed him instantly, seemingly worse than ever.

"Want something to drink with that sandwich, Dear?" She reached into the refrigerator and pulled out a beer.

"No thanks, Mom. And school's out, remember?" Jack remembered the conversation between he and Meagan. He shrugged his shoulders.

"Mom?"

"Oh, that's right. I was with some of our friends." She grabbed a bag of opened Ruffles and the bottle of beer she had retrieved from the refrigerator and sat down opposite Jack.

Jack smelled alcohol on her breath, but his Mother seemed okay.

"Uh, I was wondering, uh." Geez, why was it so difficult to form the words? Why could he not just tell her what he was thinking and feeling. Jack stared at the sandwich in front of him, his appetite had totally disappeared.

"Well? What?" She took a long draw on her beer bottle. "Ah!" She set the bottle on the table with a loud knock and looked at her son.

"I, uh."

"What is it? Just say it. Don't tell me you got to go to summer school. Don't tell me that!"

Jack shook his head without looking up.

"Got kicked off the football team?" She shrugged her shoulders as if that wouldn't be such a big deal.

Jack shook his head again.

"Naw. Nothing about school, Mom. Football practice starts in August like I said, and I am sure you'll see all good grades when the report card gets here."

"Oh, okay. Well, I'm not playing the guessing game, Jack. What is it?! Are you having a problem with one of your friends or something? Or don't tell me you have a girlfriend!"

Her stern voice sent a shiver down his spine and he could feel thousands of goose bumps cover his arms. Jack felt like all the hairs on his arms were standing straight up.

"No, no, no, Mom." He shook his head slowly. "I was wondering, could I talk to you, and Dad, you know, just kind of talk about things."

She looked at him quizzically. She was about to place a chip into her open mouth and stopped, pulled it back out and stared at Jack.

"Of course you can talk to us. About what things?" She took another long draw from her bottle, which left it empty. Then she lit up a cigarette.

"Well. I, uh, I mean it's about those, for one," pointing at her cigarette.

"These? Cigarettes? You want to start smoking, do you?" She shook her head.

"No, no, Mom." A dark cloud assembled in his head, the thunder rumbled and just like that, the words rained out.

I don't like them. I mean; they stink; they stink up the whole house, and they make you smell bad, too."

The words came out in a scolding voice he wasn't used to using and Jack cringed somewhat waiting for the response, lowering his eyes to the table. When silence followed he slowly raised his eyes up to meet his Mother's.

She stared at him, anger in her eyes. Jack knew it. She was going to put him in his place, tell him no punk kid was going to tell her what to do in her own house. But instead she kept repeating the last thing he said in her head. *And they make you smell bad, too.* Her face softened.

He told me I stink. His Mother stinks. Her heart felt like it had been stabbed. She put out her half smoked cigarette.

"What else?" She said with a frog in her throat.

"You and Dad argue a lot. I hear you in the bedroom. You're different when you fight. You're not nice. Neither one of you. You're all right when you don't fight, but when you do, you're different. You make me feel bad a lot."

"Well, we, we work hard trying to give you a nice home, put food on the table, give you an education, clothes..."

Jack nodded but didn't say anything. His eyes returned to his uneaten sandwich.

His Mother's eyes became slightly watery. She knew she was making excuses for herself. She looked at her son, his head down showing her his sandy straight hair. She became angry again.

"Anything else, Mr. Know It All?" Her voice was shaky.

"They say it's really difficult to stop smoking. I've been reading up on it. You can get help. Uh, there are things like patches and gum, and there are places, you know, that help people who want to quit but can't."

"People like what? Me? Your Dad? Are you saying we are addicts? That we need help? Is that it? They're just cigarettes, not drugs!" The anger continued to grow in her voice. "You better not tell your Dad what you told me! He'll, he'll, you know."

"Get mad."

"Yes."

"Like you are now!" Jack said the words slowly and deliberately, his eyes glued to his sandwich.

Jack's heart felt like someone was squeezing it so tight it hurt. His eyes watered but he fought back the tears. His whole face began to feel like it was on fire. Something, everything, from deep down inside him rumbled and then erupted. Then Jack surprised himself.

"I'm so tired of being afraid of you all!" He screamed at her. Then he jumped up, ran to his bedroom, slammed the door, and rolled onto the bed. Jack curled up in a fetal position and closed his eyes as tight as he could, hoping everything would just go away. His whole body shook as he sobbed violently.

He didn't understand what he was feeling. Everything seemed too much. His parents, the adventure, Meagan, the Magic Pond. All of it seemed to be a huge weight on him, pinning him down. He could barely breathe.

Jack waited, expecting his Mother to barge into the room, but the minutes passed and nothing happened. After a short time. Jack sat up, wiping the tears from his wet face, still half expecting his Mother to appear in the doorway. Had he made a mistake? Would she tell his Father? If she did, he would certainly get in trouble. His stomach felt nauseous.

We both said it wasn't going to be easy, Meagan. And it's not. I think I blew it. I hope you don't. Girls are usually smarter at talking. I wish you were here to talk to. Somehow, Jack felt better talking to Meagan even if she wasn't here with him.

How was he going to face his Father? There had to be an easier way. Well he did it, anyway, right or wrong. He was proud of himself for finally saying something. At least he was able to tell his Mother how he felt and what he had been thinking for so very long. There was some relief in getting some of the nagging issues of his chest. But Jack was still scared that it might make things worse.

"You have mail" blinked on the monitor. Jack rose and opened the email. It was a friend from school inviting him to a challenge on a computer game. He declined. His present problems erased any desire to compete on the computer, at least for now. Jack replied that he would try to compete tomorrow.

He began exploring the internet, how to stop smoking and drinking. The information was overwhelming. Getting the information was easier than he thought, though sifting through the volumes of data would be work. He wanted to be prepared, to have answers for his parents, like he always seemed to find for his friends.

CHAPTER 11

Facing Dad

Sometimes when you think it'll be tough
And the road to success seems rough
You discover you were amiss
And life, once again, becomes bliss

"Jack, can you come downstairs? "

Uh-oh. Dad is home. Time to face the music. Jack sighed heavily, climbed out of his chair and shut down the computer. Maybe he would be banned from using it for a while, no playing games with his friends.

"Coming, Dad." He glanced outside. It was dark. He slowly descended the stairs.

Jack's Mother and Father were sitting on the couch. Jack approached them resignedly.

"Hi Jack," his Father said with authority, which made Jack's stomach turn into a knot. Franklin and

Caroline occupied the sofa and Jack's Father nodded at the single chair to his left for Jack to sit.

"I understand you yelled at your Mother earlier," he began. Jack felt his eyes boring a hole through him.

"He was upset, Dear," his Mother began, but Franklin raised his hand to stop her.

"You always defend him. Then I have to put order back into this house." He turned back to his son. "First of all, we never raise our voice to our parents, understand?"

"Yes, sir. I apologize, Mom. I just…"

"Stop. You can soft talk your Mother but not me. If you have something to say, you just say it. I'm not an ogre. Now your Mother tells me you told her she 'stinks'." A slight smile crept to Franklin's lips, but he fought it back, but not before Jack caught it. Franklin nodded. "Understood. This house should be a clean habitat for you, and all of us, to live in, so from now on, all smoking will be done outside. As far as the drinking goes, it's really none of your business what your Mother and I do when we go out. We don't come home intoxicated, and we don't come home in the wee hours of the morning. Neither one of us shirks our responsibilities to this family."

"Yes, sir." *Smoking outside was progress, wasn't it? Little at a time, right?*

"Good, now that we got that straight, I thought maybe I'd take everyone out to eat. "Isn't Perry's Lobster House your favorite?"

Jack nodded slowly. He was confused. Their faces were both happy faces. Their smiles were so big they showed their teeth.

"Good. Let's go then. I bet you're just a little hungry by now. I sure am."

"He's always hungry, Dear, and he never ate that big sandwich he made earlier." His Mother chuckled and winked at Jack.

"I remember when I was his age, my father called me a human garbage disposal. There were never any leftovers," Jack's Father commented.

Perry's Lobster House was a huge red barn type structure that had many little rooms of six tables instead of one huge floor. They gave you a small bucket of peanuts in their shells when you sat down and you actually were supposed to throw the shells on the floor. Jack loved doing that. He certainly wasn't allowed to do that at home. His Mother and Father, of course, collected their shells on a plate and when the bucket was empty, which Jack always made sure happened, they would transfer the shells into the bucket and give it to the waitress. Most of the time, the server simply dumped them on the floor. That was one of the highlights of coming to this restaurant for Jack.

"So what will it be, Champ? By the way, don't worry about football. I'll make sure our vacation doesn't interfere," his father said.

Jack glanced at his Mother who was smiling.

"Cool, Dad. Thanks. Can I have the shrimp plate?"

"Sure. And you, Dear?"

"The sirloin."

"Medium, right? Loaded potato? Ranch dressing on the salad?"

"You remembered," she poked him softly in the ribs with her elbow.

"Well, it's lobster for me. I mean, this is a lobster house, right?"

The waitress came and took their orders.

"Now," his Father began. "Your Mother and I have been thinking. You shouldn't be afraid to talk with us. You never used to be. Both, she and I have been very busy, and haven't really been spending much time with you, not quality time, anyway. My guess is that to you, it seems we only complain and discipline you.

"So I figured. It's summer; no school; no home-work; June and July. August you start football prac-tice. So how about we make some weekend trips, like fishing in Galveston, Lake Texarkana, or Freemont. I can't really take a whole week off work, but I can get a Friday or Monday here and there to make it a long weekend. Your Mother says she can do the same."

"Great Dad! Can I bring a friend?"

"Of course. Red, I assume?"

Jack nodded. His Mother frowned. She didn't like that idea, but then she and Franklin would be chaper-oning them.

"And then I thought maybe, if time allows me, I'd teach you how to play golf. Hell, you're tall enough now to handle the clubs. What do you say?"

"Super!"

"But you learn on a driving range first. When you can hit the ball with every swing, I'll take you out on the course."

"Don't worry, Dad. I won't embarrass you. I'll probably end up beating you."

"Yeah. Sure. Dream on, Son."

Father and son laughed in unison.

Dinner turned out to be one of the most enjoyable meals of the year for Jack. He just couldn't remember being any happier. He had made progress. He didn't get everything he wanted, but that was okay. Tomorrow was another day, right? Little by little. The golf idea was a real extra, something he had never thought about.

Jack would have a great summer, but fall and the start of school would bring Jack new problems, problems that would be more challenging, adventures that would test his friendship to the max with his best friend, and adventures that would, once again, get him into trouble with his parents, and the police.

ABOUT THE AUTHOR

Perry DeFiore is the author of many science fiction titles, and a former Junior High School Principal in a private school in Monterrey, Mexico, as well as a teacher at the Technological University of Monterrey. He holds various diplomas in adolescent psychology, with additional studies from a California Bible College. DeFiore has traveled extensively instructing teachers on how to teach math and science to teens. He wrote more than fifty textbooks for private schools and worked with American publishers of textbooks in instructing teachers.

DeFiore has a passion for sciences, which led him to study Ocean Sciences at the University of Wisconsin, Environmental Sciences at the University of Connecticut, and Electricity and Mechanics at the Cleveland

Institute. In his writing career he completed his studies at the New York Institute, specializing in fiction. As a writer and learning enthusiast DeFiore still continues his education, currently taking courses in Human Behavior and writing. Through his education and life experiences DeFiore loves to build worlds that bring a rich knowledge into tantalizing fiction. He lives in Texas with his wife, Blanca, who lovingly refers to him as a permanent student.

Jack's next adventure, **Falling in the Hands of Evil**, finds him in a really difficult spot when he tries to help his friend Red escape a gang of boys at school who recruit adolescents to do their dirty work for them. Jack, himself, gets pulled into serious trouble.